LEVI COFFIN
and the
Underground
Railroad

LEVI COFFIN
and the
Underground
Railroad

Charles Ludwig

HERALD PRESS
Scottdale, Pennsylvania
Kitchener, Ontario
1975

Library of Congress Cataloging in Publication Data

Ludwig, Charles, 1918-
   Levi Coffin and the Underground Railroad.

   1. Coffin, Levi, 1798-1877 — Fiction. 2. Underground railroad — Fiction. I. Title.

PZ3.L96743Le   [PS3523.U434]   813'.5'2   75-12583
ISBN 0-8361-1770-0

LEVI COFFIN AND THE UNDERGROUND RAILROAD
Copyright © 1975 by Herald Press, Scottdale, Pa. 15683
   Published simultaneously in Canada by Herald Press,
   Kitchener, Ont. N2G 1A7
Library of Congress Catalog Card Number: 75-12583
International Standard Book Number: 0-8361-1770-0
Printed in the United States of America
Design by Alice B. Shetler

For Robert Huff
Chairman of the committee which restored
the Coffin House in Fountain City
and to
Mrs. Howard E. Laughlin and Miss Opal Thornburg
who cochaired the Furnishings Committee

CONTENTS

PREFACE

Few periods in American history have been as exciting as those prior to the War Between the States. During these fifty to seventy-five years, an ever increasing stream of slaves was perpetually trying to work itself to the North — and freedom.

In making his way north, the slave faced terrifying hazards. He was pursued by professional slave-catchers armed with guns and bloodhounds. His description was displayed in post offices and other public buildings along with the rewards offered for his capture. The slave — and those who would help him — were faced with prosecution under the Fugitive Slave Laws of 1793 and 1850. These laws were brazenly on the side of the masters. But the slave-catchers and the law were not the only problems faced by the runaways. Most of the slaves were penniless and illiterate. This meant they could not buy food on the way, nor could they read maps.

The slaves soon learned, however, that if they kept edging toward the North Star, they would eventually — perhaps in six months or a year — get to freedom. But on the way they faced the perils experienced by an animal escaped from the zoo. Traveling only at night through strange lands and sometimes alligator-infested swamps, the fugitives never knew when they would be discovered and clapped into the nearest jail for the benefit of their master.

The one bright light gleaming from the keyhole of the locked door was the Underground Railroad. This railroad was not a conventional one. Instead, it was a series of houses along the way where a slave's midnight rap would open the door, supply him with food, clothing, and transportation to the next "depot" twenty to thirty miles to the north.

Those courageous men who operated the Underground Railroad were in constant jeopardy of heavy fines or imprisonment — and occasionally both. Indeed, many went to prison and served long sentences. Others escaped prison but were financially ruined.

Prominent among the operators was Levi Coffin. And so successful was he, the slave-catchers sneered at him as the *President of the Underground Railroad*. Along with his energetic wife, Katie, Levi personally assisted more than two thousand slaves on their way to freedom.

Among the slaves he helped was Eliza Harris — the Eliza of *Uncle Tom's Cabin* who crossed the Ohio on heaving slabs of ice. In fact, Harriet Beecher Stowe used the Coffins as the models for Rachel and Simeon Halliday in her famous book.

10

Today a vast amount of material is available on the Underground Railroad. Thus, it is unnecessary to list sources for those who wish to go into the subject in depth. But I must mention that I received major help from Levi Coffin's autobiography, *Reminiscences of Levi Coffin*. This is a key book for those who would study this era.

Also I am grateful for the help I received from Miss Opal Thornburg, Archivist of Earlham College. Miss Thornburg pointed out and lent useful books from the Quaker collection, and helped me obtain photocopies of some of Levi Coffin's private papers — and of a source that has never before appeared in English except in limited bulletins.

Thanks must also go to Robert N. Huff who worked with others in restoring Levi Coffin's home in Fountain City. He not only made a special trip to show me through the home, but was faithful in answering all of my letters.

Charles Ludwig
March 1975

DANGEROUS
MISSION

YOUNG Levi Coffin's heart bubbled with a strong mixture of fear and pity as he dragged his feet toward Doctor Caldwell's palatial home. So much — so very much — depended on him! And yet even before he walked up the drive his feet seemed like rocks. What would he say?

Levi's one splinter of hope was that when he carefully explained the matter, Doctor Caldwell would have a twinge of mercy. But he feared that this was too much to expect, for the Reverend Doctor was a slaveholder — and his own slave was the center of the problem.

The laws of North Carolina, dealing with those who aided runaways, were severe. Levi knew of a number of men who had been arrested for doing exactly what his parents had done. And this was the reason the chills were swooshing down his spine. Brave as he was, he

13

hated to walk up those final steps and knock at the big door. Still, he didn't want his parents to be summoned to court; and so he clamped his teeth shut like a man mounting the gallows and forced himself to keep going.

As hard as it was, he knew it was the only way.

Levi didn't blame anyone for his predicament. After all, it was entirely his own fault for having volunteered to go and negotiate. Like most Coffins, Levi and his parents were God-fearing Quakers who loathed slavery in all its forms. Although they had a horror of breaking civil law, they found it more satisfactory to "obey God rather than men." Indeed, they were quite willing to suffer any penalty the state or nation might inflict in order to remain firm in their convictions.

Quakers had been hanged for their convictions, and the Coffins did not feel they should be more favored than other believers.

None of this hearty clan went out of the way to find trouble. But trouble found them in much the same manner that a moth finds the light. Frequently it squirmed into their lives in the most unexpected ways. And that is exactly how they had gotten mixed up with Ede.

Soon the dreaded Caldwell home was in sight. As Levi forced himself forward, the whole affair came back to him in grim outline.

AT BEDTIME, Prudence Coffin had been ready to blow out the candle in the living room when there was a series of frantic knocks at the door.

Carefully, she cracked the door just wide enough to see. There in the darkness, half-hidden in the shadows, stood a tall black woman. She was wearing an ankle-

14

length calico dress. A little girl was riding on her hip.

"Yes?" asked Mrs. Coffin, cautiously through the crack.

"Please, Missis," said the half-sobbing slave on the path, "I-I don't want to get you into trouble with the law, but I'm c-cold and greatly a-feared my little Mary is dyin'. Could I — "

"Of course you are welcome," said Mrs. Coffin as she pulled the woman inside and quickly locked the door.° Then, after pointing the woman to a chair, she carefully drew all the blinds. "You don't have to explain anything here," she assured the woman. "All slaves are welcome in our home. But how long has it been since you've had something to eat?"

"I guess I did a foolish thing," mumbled the woman, forcing the words beyond her thick lips with some difficulty. "When I learned that Massa was a-goin' to separate me from my children and give me to his preacher-son in de southern part of the state, I just ran off and hid in de woods."

"But how long has it been since you've had something to eat?" repeated Mrs. Coffin.

"Oh, I dunno. Mebbe a week."

"A week!" exclaimed the woman of the house. "Then don't tell me anything more until I get you and the baby a hot meal."

Within moments Prudence Coffin was blowing the coals into a blaze with leather bellows. An expert at assembling meals for unexpected guests, she didn't waste a move. Soon the kettles and frying pan were heating

---

° For easier reading, we are substituting normal English for the quaint "thee's" and "thou's" of old-time Quaker talk.

and she was reaching for ingredients.

As the spicy aroma began to fill the kitchen, the Coffin family drifted in to watch and listen.

"And who is your massa, Ede?" asked Levi, Sr., for by now the entire household had learned her name.

"Massa Caldwell."

"You mean Doctor Caldwell, the preacher?" asked Prudence, a little startled.

"That's right. And he am a mighty fine man. But his wife am even better. When she l'arned that Massa was a-gonna give me away she began to plead for me. And my, how that woman did plead. You should have heard her! Her eyes got so big and tender I thought that sure 'nuff they was a-gonna melt. She said it warn't right for me to be separated from my husband and three children. But Massa argued that my husband wasn't much good that I warn't legally married to him and that after he done give me away I'd find a much better husband. But still I was mighty thankful that Massa Caldwell was willin' for me to keep the baby. As I said, he's a mighty fine man. And he's a good preacher, too!"

Suddenly Ede was crying. "My husband ain't no cyclone for work," she sobbed. "But he's a good man — and he's a Christian. And I don't want no other nohow."

"What are your present plans?" asked Prudence. She filled Ede's cup with a twisting stream of amber coffee from her battered pot and brought a mug of warm milk for the baby.

"Well, I knows that Preacher Caldwell is a good man," said Ede as she spoon-fed her baby. "He really knows the Bible and he's good to his slaves. It's been a long time since he whipped any of us. I just hate to leave him. I thought that mebbe if I stayed away for a week or two he'd have time to think it over and mebbe decide to keep me. I've worked hard and I've been a good slave. I'd like nothin' better than to return to him — if he'd let me stay."

The baby began to cry, and Prudence did what she could to make her comfortable. The weary days in the damp thicket had been too much. Little Mary's cheeks were thin. The tiny red ribbons on her pigtails were askew and soiled with the blackness of the marsh. But having raised seven children of her own, Prudence had a way with babies.

"Now you go to bed," she said to Ede. "I'll take care of Mary."

The baby didn't settle into sleep until early in the morning. When Prudence laid her on the bed in the arms of her mother, she was still wheezing.

THE ELDER Levi's face was creased with worry as he spoke to his family around the table. "Now we must decide what to do," he said. "As everyone knows, it is against the law in North Carolina to harbor a fugitive — and that's exactly what we've done."

"But if we hadn't taken her in she and Mary might have died," said young Levi.

"True," replied the father. "But the law is the law. And what we've done may be discovered any moment. We've been under suspicion for a long time. Every slaveholder in Guilford County knows that we've been sending food to the fugitives. And those people are just waiting for an excuse to prosecute us. Nothing would

17

please them better than to drive every Friend out of the state! The patrol goes around every three weeks. It's legal for them to whip any Negro they find away from their owner's place unless they have a pass. The patrol is keeping its eyes open for all of those who help the slaves."

"I think the best idea is to go to Doctor Caldwell and tell him the truth," said Prudence. "Ede wants to return to him. And if she does, that will be the end of the matter."

"We still broke the law," said the elder Levi.

"And what if Caldwell insists on giving her to his son?" asked the younger Levi.

"Well, whoever goes over to see him will have to persuade the old man not to send her away," said Prudence. "According to the law, she's his property and he can do to her just about anything he pleases."

"Mother's right," said Levi, Sr. With a hurried glance at his pocket watch, he added, "We will have to have a volunteer. I have some business in Greensboro and will need to be gone all day."

Young Levi studied the faces of his parents, and especially those of his sisters. No one made the slightest move. From outside he could hear the wind blowing through the trees. Inside, the ticking of the grandfather clock in the living room sounded like hammerblows.

Finally, young Levi raised his hand. "I'll go," he said.

"Excellent," replied his father. "I think you can do the job. That smile of yours is hard to resist. But before you go, you should have some idea what to say. Listen carefully."

He got up and peered out the window, a look of deep concern on his face. Then he smiled. "I heard a buggy and thought it might be the patrol. But it isn't. It's just Friend Henry who's going to Greensboro with me." His face resumed its furrowed expression.

"No one around here is quite as famous — or as powerful — as Doctor Caldwell," he continued thoughtfully. "During the Revolution the British plundered his house and burned his library. And during the terrible battle of Guilford Courthouse, he was out helping the people. And so he's a hero.

"You must be very diplomatic. If he gets angry with us, all he'd have to do would be to say the word and every Friend in New Garden would have to leave."

"What will happen if I fail and he has you and Mother arrested?" asked young Levi.

"The law says that we'd have to pay a heavy fine to the owner of the slave in addition to the damages. We might even be sent to jail."

"That's terrible!"

"Of course it is. But if you follow my advice there's no need to get into any trouble." He stopped abruptly and asked one of the girls to invite Friend Henry into the house. Then he went on. "Remember Doctor Caldwell is a brilliant man. He started the first college in North Carolina — and five of his students became state governors. That's quite a record. Now don't argue with him — especially about slavery."

"But I'll have to convince him," said young Levi. "I've talked to him before and I know his ways. What will I do if he starts quoting the Bible?"

"Just don't let him lead you astray. The best two

Scriptures to use are Deuteronomy 23:15, and the story of the Good Samaritan.

"Now I know you are familiar with the story of the robbers and the Good Samaritan. But what did Moses have to say in Deuteronomy?"

"That's easy," replied Levi promptly. "Thou shalt not deliver unto his master the servant which is escaped from his master unto thee," he quoted with confidence.

"Excellent! That's powerful Scripture. Caldwell will have trouble answering that. Levi, Sr., started to open the door, and then he hesitated, his hand on the latch. "Try not to talk to him about Ede unless his wife is present. Rachel has a tender heart. The students used to say, 'Doctor Caldwell teaches the scholars, and Mrs. Caldwell teaches the ministers.' "

"Should I talk off my hat when I enter his house?"

"What? Pay him that honor? Never! Never!"

"Friend Jonathan Greene takes off his hat in public buildings."

"Yes, and Friend Jonathan believes other things no true Friend should believe. I'm an old-fashioned Friend just like George Fox. I'll never compromise. Never. Not even if they hang me!"

WITH HIS heart beating a tattoo and his hat firmly ensconced on his head, Levi knocked at the massive door. A moment later, a light-colored slave in scarlet livery invited him inside.

"I-I came to s-see Doctor Caldwell. It's important," gulped Levi.

"Just this way, Mas'r Levi. But ain't yo' gonna take off yo' hat?"

20

"No, no. I-I guess not. I'm a Friend. We only take our hats off to God."

Doctor Caldwell was writing a letter at his desk when Levi entered.

"I'm sure glad to see you," said Caldwell, pulling out a cane-bottomed chair. "And please tell me how Jeremiah Hubbard is making out at the New Garden School."

"He's doing very well. Everyone likes him. Especially the children," said Levi, trying desperately to sound calm.

"Well, you know, I think you ought to pay Hubbard double tuition. I've heard that in addition to the regular subjects he's teaching the art of courting."

A little relaxed by this banter, Levi's confidence began to rise. Still he was determined not to broach the subject until Rachel was present.

Suddenly Caldwell's face became stern. "Since you're here," he said, fixing him with a stare in much the same way that a boy would pin a butterfly, "I want you to tell me something."

"Yes. I-I mean. What."

The Reverend Doctor shifted uneasily in his chair and then leaned forward. "Please, can you tell me why the Quakers are always theeing and thouing everyone."°

"That's simple. In England in the middle 1600s, those pronouns were used in addressing servants and anyone below one's social class. But, you see, Friends don't believe in social distinctions. That's why I don't call you 'sir' too."

"And is that why you don't take off your hat —

° See the footnote on page 15.

even in the house?"

"Yes, that's why. We only take our hats off to God. You see, we believe all men are equal before God."

Caldwell's manner now became even more solemn. "You Quakers think that you can solve all of the problems of the world — even the problems of slavery!" He pulled a magazine from the desk drawer and pointed a thick finger at a column of figures. "What is the population of North Carolina?" he asked, speaking like a teacher giving a final.

"I-I really don't know," stammered Levi.

"Well, in 1810 — and that wasn't very long ago — the white population was 376,410. And what do you think the slave population is?" he demanded, lifting a bushy eyebrow.

"I don't know that either."

"The colored population," said Caldwell, wagging a finger under Levi's nose "is 168,824! And that means there are almost half as many blacks in our state as whites. Now what would happen if the slaves got dissatisfied and started a war like they did in Santo Domingo — or took off for Canada?"

"I'm sure I don't know," said Levi uncomfortably.

"If that happened our state would collapse. We'd all be finished. Finished. I said. Finished! That's the reason we have the patrol. The slaves must obey their masters. You Quakers need to learn that slavery is ordained of God. Abraham had slaves!"

The hollow spot that had been forming in Levi's stomach was getting bigger all the time. He was tempted to excuse himself and leave. But the memory of Ede and her baby riveted him to his seat.

22

"I have something v-very important to s-say to you, Doctor Caldwell," stammered Levi.

"Well, let's hear it."

"M-maybe it would be better if your wife was present."

"Oh, so it's really important!" said Caldwell, his eyebrow rising.

He shook a tiny brass bell on his desk. When the slave in scarlet appeared, he said, "Tell Rachel to come to the study."

A bright smile crossed Mrs. Caldwell's face as she took a seat next to her husband.

"I came to see you about Ede," gulped Levi.

"And what's the trouble with Ede?" snapped Caldwell, leaning forward.

"Well, she and her baby are over at our house. Mother —"

"You know the law is hard on those who harbor fugitives," said Caldwell sternly, interrupting him.

"Yes, so I've heard. But you should know the whole story before you pass judgment." Levi related what had happened, emphasizing that his mother had probably saved little Mary's life.

As he spoke, Levi could see a look of sympathy in Mrs. Caldwell's eyes. Encouraged, he summoned all his will power. Looking the preacher straight in the face, he said, "Doctor Caldwell, I know you have preached about the Good Samaritan. Now tell me, did Mother do the right thing?"

Caldwell and his wife exchanged glances. The former college president said, "You did the right thing. But the truth is that we didn't want to harm Ede. All

23

we did was give her to my son Sam, the pastor at
Sugar Creek. Of course that would have separated her
from her children and that lazy husband of hers. What
Ede needs is a good flogging for her foolishness!"

Levi quoted Deuteronomy 23:15.

Doctor Caldwell flushed. "You've done your home-
work, young man. If you will tell her to return to us
I'd appreciate it. Please assure her that we will
allow her to remain with us."

Relieved of his anxiety, Levi thanked the Caldwells
and stood to leave. "Not so fast," said the Doctor, waving him back to his seat. "This no doubt was your first
sermon, and you were quite successful. I think you
would make a pretty good preacher. If you'd like to
study theology, you can come over here and I'll give
you lessons — free."

WHEN EDE learned about Doctor Caldwell's decision,
she clapped her hands and shouted again and again,
"Praise de Lord!" Praise de Lord!" Toward the middle
of the afternoon, Prudence Coffin presented her with a
blanket for the baby and sent her back to Doctor Caldwell.

Levi was rejoicing in what he had accomplished when
Catherine White galloped up on her little mare.

"I heard that you were over to see Doctor Caldwell," said Catherine smiling down at him.

"And how did such news get clear over to Hopewell," said Catherine, smiling down at him from her
sidesaddle position.

"A wee little bird told me," she teased, flashing
white even teeth.

Levi escorted her into the living room and seated her by the grandfather clock.

"It's wonderful to know someone who hates slavery as much as I do," she said. Then she removed her starched bonnet and hung it on a peg. "Some of the Friends at Hopewell think that slavery is all right. But I don't. I think it is of the devil. And so does Father!"

Gleefully, Levi related his encounter with the Caldwells. Then he added, "You know, Katie, he thinks slavery is advocated in the Bible. I wouldn't be surprised he thinks Ede sinned by running away."

Changing the subject, Levi said, "I think I'll ride over to Hopewell on First Day. I'd like to visit your father."

"That will be great," said Catherine. "We'll see you at the meetinghouse."

Levi enjoyed Catherine's spunk. Although she was younger than himself, she had the courage of George Fox and William Penn all rolled together. In addition, she was a good cook!

Before moving to Hopewell, the Whites had been close neighbors to the Coffins in New Garden. Both families had been Friends for at least two generations.

LEVI BECOMES AN
ABOLITIONIST

THE WORD "abolitionist" was practically unknown in the early 1800s. Even so, young Levi began to adopt abolitionist principles long before he had shed his last baby teeth. And this was a full quarter of a century before the despised epithet came into general use.

The two incidents that pushed him into the conviction that slavery must be abolished were sudden and dramatic. While a mere seven, Levi was standing near the Salisbury Road watching his father chop wood when he heard the sound of a clanking chain.

Peering down this road where much of the Revolutionary battle of Guilford Court House had been fought, he noticed a column of black men approaching. The men had been handcuffed in pairs. A grim chain, locked to each set of manacles, continued down the entire length of the line. Riding behind — a week's growth of red whiskers surrounding his lopsided mouth — was a white man on a wagon loaded with supplies. The man carried a long whip which he waved and snapped from time to time.

Intrigued, young Levi sidled up to his father as the gang drew near. "Well, boys, why have they chained you?" asked the elder Coffin.

"Because we've been kidnapped," replied an intelligent looking black. "They're afraid we'll escape and return to our families."

After the clink-clank, clink-clank of the chain had faded, Levi slipped his hand into his father's and asked, "Did they do something bad?"

"No, son," replied his father, his voice edged with anger.

"Then why have they been chained? And why does that bad man on the wagon shake his whip at them as if they are animals?"

"Because he is taking them to an auction for sale."

"Like we sell pigs and horses?" asked Levi, looking intently into his father's face.

"Yes, just like we sell pigs and horses."

"But some of those black men are fathers and they have boys and girls just like my sisters and me." He was thoughtfully silent for a long time, then added in a husky voice, "I know you wouldn't want to leave us —"

"That makes no difference to a slaver. All those greedy people want is money — and more money! But let's hurry home. It's time to eat."

As they returned to New Garden, young Levi kept wondering how he would feel if someone chained his father and drove him with a cattle whip to an auction. Such thoughts troubled him greatly.

Sometime later, Levi went with his father to the Yadkin River where the stream breaks through a spur in the mountains and plunges wildly through a series of rapids. In the spring, shad fought their way up the river to spawn. While on their way upstream, these delicious two- and three-pound fish were easily caught and in great demand.

There was a camp at the rapids owned by the Crump brothers where people normally came to trade for fish. But since there were so many, the brothers allowed their slaves to catch the shad at night, sell them, and keep the money.

After buying several fish from a slave, Levi and his son made camp for the night. In the morning, while they were cooking fish over an open fire and eating them for breakfast, the slave who had sold the shad sauntered up.

"How do you like them?" he asked in a friendly way.

"They're fine," said the elder Coffin.

"I have plenty. Would you like some more at the same price?"

Coffin was about to reply when a nephew of the Crumps strode up.

Grabbing the slave by the shoulder, he whirled him around. "What do you mean, talking to the white men like that?" he snarled.

"I only asked if they like the fish," the youth said.

"Well, remember that you're just a nigger-slave, and you're supposed to keep your trap shut." Then he grabbed a burning fagot and smashed him over the head. "Maybe that'll teach you not to be so impertinent!" he shouted.

"You shouldn't do such things," said Coffin, angrily. "The lad may be a slave. But he's also a human being!"

"Ah, they're all the same," stormed the man after a volley of unprintable oaths.

A hurried examination showed that the youth's scalp had been cut to the bone. Coffin would have dressed his wound. But he had no supplies. As the youth staggered away, his face was drenched with blood.

Heartsick, young Levi could eat no more. He fled to a secluded spot where he burst into uncontrollable tears. On their way home, Levi said, "Father, I'm going to give my life to stop such things. That nephew of the Crumps should be put in jail! I wonder what Jesus would have done had He been there."

"I'm glad to hear you speak so," said his father, drawing him up close on the buggy seat. "Slavery is a terrible sore and every Friend should work to stop it."

THE COFFINS were a determined people and they could trace their ancestors back to 1066! That was the year Sir Richard Coffin accompanied William the Conqueror from Normandy on his famous invasion of England. As a reward for his bravery, Sir Richard was given the manor at Alwington in the country of Devonshire.

In the centuries that followed, historians dipped their quills many times in order to write about one Coffin or another — many of whom were distinguished knights. In 1642 Tristram Coffyn — some spelled it this way — moved across the Atlantic to Salisbury, Massachusetts. Then, along with eight other men, he purchased Nantucket Island from the Indians. But the island, just off the coast of Massachusetts, was not very fertile; and so, just prior to the Revolution, a large group — belonging to the Society of Friends — moved from the island to Guilford County in North Carolina.

Levi's grandparents, William and Priscilla Coffin, were among those who moved. They settled at New Garden and earned their living on a farm.

Their home was known for its hospitality. Frequently traveling elders and others from the Society of Friends stayed with them. They had ten children, including eight sons. Levi's father was the youngest of the sons.

Levi Coffin married Prudence Williams whose parents had donated the land for the New Garden Meetinghouse. Levi was a hardworking and studious farmer who was constantly reading. One winter he taught school in the New Garden community. Seven children were born to them; all but one were girls. Levi, the only son, was next to the youngest. He was born in New Garden in 1798.

Concerning himself, this younger Levi wrote: "My father took pains to instruct me and my sisters during his hours of leisure from outdoor work so that I kept even with my associates in the neighborhood who had better opportunities for gaining an education, and during the short intervals that I attended school, I was classed with them, and often stood at the head of the class."

AT BREAKFAST, Levi, Sr., turned to his son. "I heard that you are going to Hopewell on First Day. Be sure and give my regards to Stanton White and his wife. They are true Friends. But I think that before you go, you should take Blackie to the blacksmith. This morning I noticed that she's about to lose her left front shoe."

While Levi awaited his turn at the blacksmith's place in Greensboro, a slaveholder was having handcuffs forged onto the wrists of his slave — a black man in his thirties.

"Didn't we treat you well?" demanded his owner in a coarse, loud voice.

"Yes, Massa, you treated me well."

"Did you get enough to eat?"

"Yes, Massa, I got enough to eat."

"Then why did you have someone forge a pass and run away?"

"My wife and children were taken from me, Massa; and I think as much of my family as you do of yours. Their new massa wanted to buy me, too. But you refused to sell me. And so when they left, I followed."

After the blacksmith had riveted a thick iron collar around the man's neck, his owner glowered at him.

"Now tell me. Who wrote that pass?"

"I can't tell you, Massa," replied the slave, his eyes wide with terror.

In reply, the white man grabbed a hammer. "Now tell me, or I'll use this on you."

"I'm sorry, Massa, but I can't tell you."

"We'll see about that," sneered the man after he had jerked his slave to a heavy anvil near the forge. "Tell me this minute, or down comes the hammer!"

"I'm sorry, Massa. But I c-c-can't."

Livid with rage, the master struck the slave's hand

with the hammer again and again. The black man refused to even give a hint although blood darkened his nails.

At last the master gave up, for it was unprofitable for him to cripple a slave for whom he had paid good cash. But his anger was not exhausted. "I've always treated you well," he stormed. "I've trusted you with my keys. You've been more like a confidential servant than a slave. But just wait until we get home. Then you'll know what slavery *really* is!"

Almost beside himself with fury, the slaveholder seized the chain that was attached to the slave's collar and locked it onto the axle of his buggy. Then he leaped inside and lashed the horse into a trot. Trying to keep up, the slave had to run as fast as possible.

"What will happen if he can't keep up?" asked Levi.

"I dunno," replied the blacksmith. "If he can't keep up he'll either get his neck busted or some of his hide wore off."

Weak with anger, Levi started to stumble out of the shop. Then he remembered that he'd come to get Blackie shod. "It's the left front foot," he said. And then he asked, "Why did you let that man use your hammer?"

At first the blacksmith was silent. He cradled Blackie's hoof in his lap and began to pull out the nails. Finally, he said, "But, Levi, what could I do? After all, he paid good money for that slave. And the law is the law!"

THE MEETINGHOUSE at Hopewell was lined with buggies and horses when Levi trotted up, raising a cloud of dust. The yard was filled with Friends, some of whom had come many miles to worship. The women were dressed in sugar-scoop bonnets and long black or brown dresses. There were no unnecessary frills. Equally plain, the men were clad in well-made but plain black suits and were topped with broadbrims.

Soon Levi spotted Katie and her parents. Following a word of greeting, he quietly entered the building. The plain, Quaker meetinghouse was lighted by plain glass windows and furnished with plain, hard benches. In front, a line of benches faced the congregation. These were for the elders and any distant Friend who was likely to speak.

Everyone was utterly silent as they sat with their hats or bonnets on awaiting a movement of the Spirit. As each member entered, he did so with no predetermination either to speak or remain silent. Such a predetermination, it was believed, would quench the Spirit.

Suddenly an old man stood to pray. As he did so, the entire congregation rose to its feet and Levi, along with most of the men and boys, removed his hat. At the conclusion of the prayer, the congregation sat down, and the men and boys replaced their hats on their heads. Following this, there was a long silence.

Levi tried to keep the problems of slavery from his mind, but he could not. The sound of that hammer on the slave's hand kept coming before him. He looked at the worshipers about him and wondered what would happen if they all united against slavery and worked against it as a solid unit. Many Quakers in the past were powerful men. He thought of George Fox, William Penn, and Robert Barclay. Not only had Barclay been a

33

2

brilliant thinker and writer, but he had also been elected the first governor of East Jersey — even though he had never crossed the Atlantic to assume that post. All of these men had been great, and he thought of others.

The first Christian services ever to be conducted in Carolina were led by a Friend — William Edmundson in 1672. Twenty-three years later, Friend John Archdale became governor of North Carolina.

Yes, the Quakers had been strong. Moreover, they had endured. Rhode Island had had Quaker governors for thirty-six consecutive terms! Better yet, Levi rejoiced in knowing that most Friends throughout the world refused to own slaves.

Levi was thinking smugly about all of these things when an elder on the front seat abruptly shook hands with his neighbor. Soon others were doing likewise.

The service was over.

LEVI WAS in a thoughtful mood as he rode over to the Whites for dinner. On the way, Katie caught up with him. "You were so quiet this morning, were you worshiping or just thinking?" she teased.

"I was thinking," confessed Levi. "But if you had really been worshiping, you would not have noticed."

"Yes, but a body gets weary. I only watched you with one eye — and that was through my fingers!"

"Katie," said Levi, reining Blackie to a stop, "I was thinking some serious thoughts." He told her what had happened in the blacksmith's shop. "When I think of such things," he added, "my blood gets hot. Maybe God wants us — you and me and our many friends — to go on a campaign against slavery."

"You must never forget that we are gentle people," cautioned Catherine. "None of us believe in violence, and slavery is as firmly rooted in the hearts of Americans as that oak tree over there."

"I know that, Katie," said Levi, speaking slowly and weighing each word. "But slavery has to be abolished. It is wrong for one man to own another!"

"I agree," replied Catherine. She nudged her horse into a slow jog. "But how can a few of us nonviolent Quakers fight an entire government? It would be like trying to move all of these Blue Ridge Mountains with a spoon."

"We won't be trying to move the mountains with a spoon. We'll move them with faith. I don't know how. But there has to be a way."

"I am sure, Levi, that there is a way. I am also sure that you will find it. The Coffins never give up. But listen. Be careful what you say at the table. Jonathan Greene will be there, and if you speak too much about slavery, he will get bubbling angry like a pot of water on a hot stove. When he disagrees about something, he gets furious. He might even lose his wig! Besides, Mother is getting very tense."

THE LONG table was loaded with great platters of baked ham, roast beef, stuffed turkey, and shad. There were big mountains of mashed potatoes with melted butter in their craters, stacks of corn on the cob, long boats of gravy, a fruit salad, and piping hot biscuits.

"It's too much," said Levi, shaking his head.

"God has been good to us," beamed Stanton White, "and we must share His bounty."

Soon several conversations, loaded with thees and thous were being carried on simultaneously. The Friends talked about their crops, the uselessness of the recent War of 1812, the policies of President James Madison, and the fact that Indiana was about to become a state.

Levi was rejoicing that nothing had been said to antagonize Jonathan Greene, when all at once Greene pointed at him. Speaking around a large mouthful of turkey, he said, "Levi, you are too concerned with slavery. Everyone knows that your entire family has been helping the runaways. Take some advice from a Friend who has lived a long time. Leave slavery alone!"

"You sound like Cain," replied Levi, responding instantly to the challenge. "But I'm a Friend, and a good Friend is his brother's keeper."

"I don't want to argue with you, Levi," replied Greene, adjusting his wig. "But I think you should know something. After the battle of Guilford Court House, the New Garden Meetinghouse was used for a hospital for the wounded soldiers. At the time, some British officers stayed in your grandfather William's house. Then the officers got the smallpox. Instead of moving out, your grandfather treated them. The result was that he caught the disease and died."

"So?" asked Levi, his eyes flashing.

"And so he died," said Greene. "He was a good man, and if he could have stayed away from those British officers he might still be living."

"And so you think we should tolerate slavery, just as you think that you should give hat honor," replied Levi, getting to his feet. "Well, I don't. Slavery is a curse and must be abolished. That's right, abolished! If every Friend would do his duty, it would be — and soon!"

Every eye at the table was now focused on Greene and Mrs. White who was alternatingly dabbing at her eyes and blowing her nose. In an instant, moving with the quickness of a copperhead, Friend Jonathan Greene strode over to Levi. Then, after patting his wig with both hands, he jabbed his finger right under Levi's nose, and fairly hissed, "Levi Coffin, you are a troublemaker!"

"I'm sorry you feel that way," said Levi, forcing a smile. "But I have a question for you. And since you know so much about the Bible you should have an immediate answer."

"All right, let's hear it," replied Greene, calming down.

"Who was it that died before his mother was born and was buried in his grandmother's bosom?"

After several tries, Greene gave up.

"The answer is either Cain or Abel. Their mother Eve was never born. She was created. And since she was made out of Adam's rib, which was made out of earth, the earth was her sons' grandmother."

Angered by the laughter that followed, Greene shouted in a nearly hysterical voice. "I don't think the Lord likes that kind of humor. It doesn't fit in with the teachings of the Society of Friends!"

Stanton White was now on his feet. "I have an announcement," he said calmly. "Tomorrow there will be a frolic at Doctor Caldwell's. Everyone is invited. Let's all go and show that old Presbyterian how Friends can shuck corn."

Levi waited until the guests had gone. Then he apologized to Catherine for having gotten into an argument. "But I couldn't help it," he concluded lamely.

"I warned you," replied Catherine. "But, Levi, I was proud of you! You are like all the Coffins. Stubborn as a mule."

KIDNAPPED!

AS SKILLED black hands prepared the long tables where the guests would eat at the conclusion of their work, the neighbors descended on the enormous pile of corn that was heaped high in the center of the wide open space. With quick twists, eager conversation, and a song or two, they wrenched the husks from the corn. Naked ears were tossed into a nearby bin.

Since whites worked at one end of the heap and slaves at the other end, the work was soon completed.

Among the guests was Stephen Holland, a flashy neighbor who dealt in slaves. On the way from the North to the markets in the South, he had brought along the band of slaves he was going to sell. "I'll get some work out of 'em while I can," he explained.

Presently the bell clanged for supper. But fifteen-year-old Levi had decided that he would remain outside with Holland's slaves.

Almost from the start, Levi learned that one of the slaves — a teenager about his own size — claimed to be free. "But tell me, Stephen, how that could be true," he said.

"Well, you see, Massa Levi," replied the lad, "I was apprenticed to a Friend by the name of Edward Lloyd near Philadelphia, Pennsylvania. When my apprenticeship was up, a man hired me to drive his sheep to Balimore. When I got to Maryland, I went to sleep in the colored section of the hotel. During the night some men broke into my room, tied me with ropes, stuffed my mouth with rags, and then flung me into a carriage.

"They drove me across the Virginia line and locked me in a damp cellar. And was it ever damp! Big drops of water oozed out of the walls. Then they sold me to Holland. Now he's taking me South to sell at auction for a big profit. I sure hope I don't end up in the cotton fields!"

"Do you mean that the man who bought you is the man who's eating right now in the big house?"

"Yes, Massa Levi. That's him," replied Stephen with a shrug.

"This is terrible," said Levi.

"Yes, it is terrible. But, Massa Levi, this kidnapping is going on all the time. Stealing blacks and selling them in the South is big business. And the blacks are helpless, for in this land of the free a slave can't testify in court!"

AT THE corner of the table in the mansion there was an empty seat. Levi sat down there and began to eat. But soon his attention was fixed on Holland who had

become the life of the party. Dressed in the latest fashion, a diamond winked on the kerchief around his throat.
The stories he told were mostly about Negroes, and he
had a talent in imitating their dialect.

And, indeed, his tales were so funny, Levi found it
hard not to smile. In addition to talent, the man's
triple chins and hamlike arms gave him a comic appearance. In spite of his Quaker reluctance to think ill of
anyone, Levi thought Holland looked like a hog his father had once scalded in a barrel that was slightly too
small.

"What do you do for a living?" inquired a short-
sleeved farmer.

"I'm a nigger-trader."

"You mean you deal in Negroes?"

"Yep, that's my business. It's hard work and danger-
ous. Lots of travelin'. And sometimes the merchandise
gets off the hook and disappears. But the trade pays
well and I like it." He paused, licked his knife, and
used it to carve a generous supply of butter from the
main butter dish. Then as he smeared it on a thick slice
of bread, he added in a slaver-to-slaver whisper,
"Catchin' and tradin' niggers is 'bout the most excitin'
business there is." He slurped a mouthful of coffee,
churned it around in his mouth as if he were mixing
cement, and then concluded knowingly, "Of course it
ain't for everyone — 'specially if your heart's a little
mushy. Sometimes the slave mammies do a lot of
screechin' when you sell their children. But on the
whole it's a mighty satisfyin' business."

As Levi listened, he felt his hands balling into fists.
But he knew a sarcastic remark wouldn't help. Also he

41

noted that both the Caldwells were disturbed. Suddenly he remembered the preacher's slave, Tom.

Locating the trusted slave just beyond a nest of slave cabins, Levi motioned him closer and then coaxed him into the shadows.

"Tom," he whispered, "I desperately need your help."

"Yes, Massa Levi. I'll do anything to help. But I'se only a slave and can't do much," he replied, rubbing his snow-white whiskers.

Levi told him about Stephen. "Now, Tom," he confided in even a lower tone, for a trio of guests was standing nearby, "I think we can free Stephen. Here's what I want you to do. Please bring him over to our house tomorrow at midnight so that we can get the particulars of his case."

"That'll be mighty risky business," said Tom, his eyes wide.

"Yes, I know. But the Lord will be with you."

THE NEXT night Tom and Stephen showed up at the appointed time. And with the blinds drawn, Levi Coffin, Sr., wrote down the important facts about the situation. He mailed a letter to Philadelphia the following day.

Two weeks later, Hugh Lloyd, a brother of Edward, showed up — having made the trip to Greensboro by stage. But unfortunately, by this time, Stephen had already been sold in a Southern state. However, the Friends at New Garden refused to give up.

A special meeting was called in the New Garden Meetinghouse and the problem was laid before the con-

42

gregation. The Friends responded at once with an offering to finance a search for Stephen. In addition, two Friends, Doctor George Swain and Henry Macy, agreed to accompany Hugh Lloyd.

Miraculously, Stephen was found in Georgia and the case was taken to court. There, after some wrangling, and after Hugh Lloyd had returned to Philadelphia and forwarded documents which proved that Stephen's mother had been born free, he was released. The man who had kidnapped Stephen was then arrested. But since Stephen could not appear against him at the time, his friends got him out of jail on bond. Later, when Stephen was able to appear, the kidnapper fled and thus his friends forfeited their bond money.

This was the second slave Levi had helped. To Catherine, he said, "It just makes my blood tingle to know that Stephen is free and that I helped make him free. You know, there is no joy like the joy of helping people. Sometimes I think I'm walking on air. If I can, I'd like to spend the rest of my life helping slaves!"

"And so would I," agreed Catherine.

BUT THE next kidnapping that came under Levi's direct observation did not have such a happy ending. This time, the victim was the son of a Virginia slaveholder. One of this man's slaves, by whom he had a son, was a beautiful octoroon. That is, she was only one eighth Negro. And since the slaveholder was completely white, the son was thus only one sixteenth black.

For family reasons the slaveholding father, who continued to remain in Virginia, sent the son to Guilford

County to be raised. While there, the boy learned to be a shoemaker. After he had grown up, he married a white woman, raised five or six children, and joined the Methodist Church.

All went well until the slaveholder died. Then, while settling the estate, one of the sons remembered the boy who had been born to the octoroon. A quick check of the law indicated that this son was part of the estate — and could be sold!

Learning this, an heir — a half brother of the intended victim — together with an administrator — swooped down on Guilford County to claim their property. But when they arrived and learned the situation, they decided that it would be more profitable and less trouble to sell him to a dealer at a generous discount. And this they did.

Now, armed with a legally signed bill of sale, the dealer burst into the man's house to claim him. "Don't touch me! I'm no slave!" protested the astonished man.

"Oh, yes you are," snapped the dealer, "and this document proves it. Look at the signatures. I've paid good cash for you, and you are mine. You belong to me — all of you — from the top of your head to the sole of your feet! And so come with me. I'm gonna sell you at auction in New Orleans. And as smart as you are, I ought to get a ripping good price. So let's go."

Already exhausted by having sat up night after night with his extremely ill wife, the victim was not able to put up much of a struggle. Moreover, he was no match for the set of ruffians who had been hired by the trader.

The bound man was sent to the South to be sold. But

since the shrewd trader feared that his merchandise would appear to be white, he took the precaution of tying him up and leaving him in the scorching sun for a few days. The job was completed with "tan ooze." Also, his hair was shortened and curled with an iron.

In this condition, the protesting man was chained to a block and sold under the hammer to the highest bidder — a man who turned out to be a very cruel master. The slave, however, soon managed to escape. But on his return to North Carolina, he met with additional heartbreak. He learned that his wife had died of shock, and that his children had been scattered.

The desperate escapee had no time to mourn his loss, for his master appeared almost at once with bloodhounds. To avoid the dogs, he waded through a millpond and spent the night in a tree. The following day, he staggered over to the home of Stanton White. The Whites took him in, kept him out of sight, and fed him.

Sometime later, Doctor George Swain consulted a firm of attorneys about the possibility of having him declared legally free. A thorough search of the statutes indicated that this might be possible. But the dreadful ordeal of having lost his family and of hiding in the swamps was too much. The man died before the next court session.

AS YOUNG Levi worked on his father's farm, he concentrated on learning as much about slavery as possible — especially American slavery. Previous experience had shown that to be helpful to a slave he must know all of the ins and outs of the traffic — and especially the Fugitive Slave Law of 1793, then in force. Poring over book catalogs, Levi selected as many books as he could afford. Soon they began streaming into the Coffin home.

"Don't you do anything but read?" asked one of his sisters.

"Yes, I do a lot of things in addition to my reading," he said. "But these books are going to help me with my life's work. And besides that, they're interesting."

"They don't look interesting to me," sniffed the girl.

"All right, then, let me ask you a question. Did you know that less than one hundred years ago most of the people in Europe sweetened their porridge with honey and that sugar was sold by the ounce?"

"By the ounce!" she exclaimed. "Now we can buy fifty pounds at a time."

"Yes, that's right. By the ounce, just like gold. And in those days most of the sugar came from Spain. And what do you think lowered the price of sugar?"

"I haven't the slightest idea."

"Well, in 1605 the British claimed the Island of Barbados. At first they didn't do much with this territory. Then along about 1641 they began to plant sugarcane and it grew like weeds. The climate was ideal. Someone learned how to make rum out of the sugar. This increased the demand so much almost everyone went into the sugarcane business. But these greedy people forgot that they should take care of the soil. There was so much land, they didn't care. When one plantation was worn out, they started another; and when one island was exhausted, they went to the next. That's why some people call those places in the Caribbean the Sugar Islands. And did you know — "

"Look, Professor Levi," interrupted his sister, "isn't

one lesson a day enough? And besides, it's time to eat!"

"Oh, all right," grumbled Levi. Nevertheless, he took the book to the table.

Levi was hungry, for he had been hoeing in the garden. Still his passion for knowledge was even greater, and so between bites he read.

"I don't think you should read at the table," said his mother.

"Yes, I guess you're right," he replied. But after only three swallows, he faced the family, his eyes aglow. "Do you know why there was such a demand for slaves in the Sugar Islands?" he asked.

"Because they were needed to raise sugarcane and because they could endure the humid climate," replied his father.

"That's right, but did you know that from 20 to 30 percent of the slaves died on their way over from Africa and were thrown overboard?"

"I knew that a lot of them died, but I didn't know the percentage was that large," said Prudence, pausing with a spoon of peaches in midair.

"Well, you see," said Levi, speaking like an authority, "the demand for slaves in the Sugar Islands was so great and the profits were so large the captains got bigger and bigger ships. And yet that didn't satisfy them, and so they made rows and rows of bunks below. They squeezed the slaves in until they were lying together like spoons in a chest. Sometimes so many were locked down there they almost ran out of oxygen. Indeed, there were occasions when they couldn't even light a candle below the deck. It's a wonder that any survived the trip!

"And listen to what one of the plantation owners had to say — "

"Mother," shrilled the oldest girl, with her fingers in her ears, "make Levi keep still. He's ruining my pudding!"

"All right, I'll stop," said Levi. "But first I just have to read to you the statement of an overseer in Jamaica that was made to Henry Coor in 1774. Do I have permission?"

"Go ahead," said Prudence. "We're listening."

"As I said," continued Levi, speaking as rapidly as possible, "20 to 30 percent died on their way over. Then the strange climate along with the 'sunup to sundown' routine killed another 20 to 30 percent. And here is what that overseer had to say, 'I have made my employers twenty, thirty, and forth more hogsheads per year than my predecessor and though I have killed thirty to forty Negroes per year more, yet the produce has been more than adequate to the loss.' "

A long silence followed this statement. Each of the Coffins seemed preoccupied with his own thoughts, and three of the girls left their pudding untouched. As she rose to clear the table, Prudence said, "I think all of us ought to pray for the slaves."

"We also ought to pray for all those who deal in slaves and ask the Lord to have mercy on their souls," added Levi, Sr.

BEFORE going into the fields that afternoon, Levi selected some long candles and made a neat pile of his slavery books by his bed. Then with a glance at the grandfather clock he went out to mend a fence and to

48

do the chores. But even as he pounded nails into the posts and milked the cows his mind was on those books.

When he returned at sundown his mother met him at the door. "Cousin Vestal was here to see you," she said. "And by the tone of his voice, I think it's important. He seemed disappointed that you were gone."

"Why didn't you send him out to the fence I was repairing?"

"I didn't know where it was. Anyway,. he said he'll see you at the meetinghouse on First Day."

Levi paused to think. He had to decide whether he should ride Blackie over to his cousin's or stay home with the books. But it wasn't a hard decision. Although he was curious about Vestal's mission, he decided to stay home with the books!

THE SLAVE SCHOOL

LEVI WAS hitching Blackie to the rail at the meetinghouse just as Vestal Coffin trotted up. "I'm sorry I missed you," Levi said. "I was mending a fence. The cows get out, and the neighbors are upset."

"Have you ever thought of starting a slave school?" asked Vestal, getting to the point at once.

"I have," replied Levi thoughtfully. "However it's impossible. The slaveholders wouldn't allow it, and we'd be in trouble with the law."

"Most of the slaveholders wouldn't," agreed Vestal. "But I think Doctor Caldwell and his sons would — especially if we agreed to teach the slaves only to read the Bible. After the meeting, I want to show you something."

Later, they rode their horses over to the nearby brick schoolhouse. "We could get permission to use this building on First Day," said Vestal.

"Perhaps," replied Levi. Deep in thought, he rode around the building, sizing up the situation. Finally he said, "Look, Vestal, if you will get permission to use the building and help get the books, I will talk to the slaveholders. As you know, Doctor Caldwell and I are pretty good friends."

The slaveholders were a little reluctant at first. "What would happen if some of our slaves read the terrible antislavery articles that are being printed in the *Greensboro Patriot?*" asked one.

"Oh, we'll only teach them to read the Bible," countered Levi.

"Even so — " The man squirted a stream of tobacco juice at a hole in the ground, and missed. "Even so, that editor's going to get us all into trouble. Some morning all of us may have our throats slit. Remember what the slaves did in Santo Domingo? William Swaim should not be allowed to print such a sheet. If I had my way, he'd be hanged!"

"Don't worry about those things," said Levi smoothly. "I've been told that you're a deacon in the Baptist Church. Is that so?"

"Yes, that's true. I've been a deacon for more than 'leven years."

"Doesn't your Bible say that we are to teach all nations?"

"I reckon it does."

"And do you believe that the Bible teaches that slavery is right?"

"It sure does. I've heard our preacher say so again and again."

"Then wouldn't it be good if your slaves could read

51

that themselves? It would make them more content, wouldn't it?"

"Oh, all right," he grumbled. "But don't teach 'em to read nothin' but the Bible!"

The Caldwells — including the sons — and the Dokes and a few others were all agreeable, and so a date for the first session was set.

Among Doctor Caldwell's slaves was a stooped gray-head by the name of Uncle Frank. He was an accepted preacher among the slaves. When he learned of the school project, he seized both of Levi's hands in his own. "God bless you," he said. "I ain't never been to school for a single day in all my life. You and your cousin has been sent to us niggers straight from de Lord."

The slave school opened its door in the summer of 1821. Extremely curious, the slaves comfortably filled the building on the first day. "Now, before we start," said Levi, "we will ask Uncle Frank to lead us in prayer."

As the old man shuffled forward, Levi removed his hat. After the slaves had gotten to their feet, Uncle Frank lifted his hands, and turning his face heavenward began praying. His voice was husky, and as he pleaded to God for help, tears oozed from his eyes, dripped down his brown, wrinkled cheeks, and disappeared in the thicket of his beard.

His words were so solemn Levi never forgot them. Shaking his head to the rhythm of his sentences, he prayed, "I pray dat de good Massa Lord will put it in de niggers' hearts to learn to read de Good Book. Oh, Lord, make de letters in our spellin' books big and plain, and make our eyes bright and shinin', and make our hearts big and strong for to l'arn. Make our minds sharp and keen; yes, Lord, as sharp as a double-edged sword, so dat we can see clean through de Book. Oh, Hebbenly Fader, we tank De for makin' our massas willin' to let us come to dis school. And, oh Lord, do bress dese young men you has made willin' to come heah and l'arn us poor slave-niggers to read de bressed Word from de mouf of God. Oh, Lord, teach us to be good sarvents, and touch our massas' hearts and make 'em tender so dey will not lay de whips on our bare backs. And You, great Massa, shall have all de glory and praise. Amen."

Following this, Uncle Frank led them in singing "Steal Away to Jesus." As Levi thought of their plight, and considered their truly profound ability, a lump scratched at his throat. Many of these blacks had as much ability, or even more, than their masters. If only they had a chance! He found it hard to blink back the tears.

Levi and Vestal divided the slaves into small classes and began to teach them the alphabet. The slaves were so excited by this opportunity, few of them learned a thing. But they were all eager to return.

After the slaves had started back to their plantations, Levi sat next to Uncle Frank on the front seat. "I loved that song about stealing away to Jesus," he said. It was great. Who wrote it?"

"Nobody writes de songs de slaves sings," laughed Uncle Frank, showing a perfect set of teeth. "Most slaves don't even know how to write."

"Then how do they know what to sing?"

"It's a-like dis. When we're a-habbin' a meeting and somebody gets inspired, he just starts a-singin'.

Den somebody else adds new words. Den pretty soon we has a new song."

"Could you tell me how this 'Steal Away to Jesus' got started?"

"I really don't know." He arched his magnificent eyebrows as he pondered. "But dere is a story about dat song. Away down South and a little out West dere's a plantation near de Red River. Well de slaves asked dere massa permission to cross de river so dey could listen to a white preacher who come every week to gospelize de Indians. Everything was just fine and dey went every week until de massa learned dat de white preacher was from de Norf. Dat almost plumb scared him to death, for he was a-feared dat de preacher from de Norf would make de slaves want to run off and get dere freedom.

"And so de massa told de slaves dat dey couldn't go no more. And dat 'bout busted their hearts. But de slaves just couldn't stay away; and so while de slaves were a-workin in de cotton, one of 'em says to another, 'Let's steal away to Jesus.' Den after a while another slave begins to sing dem words.

"Dere were a lot of trees by de river, and so after de slaves sneaked across and dey were a-singin' about Jesus, one of 'em thought about them trees and sang, 'Green trees a-bendin', a poor sinner stands a-tremblin', de trumpet soun's it in a-my soul, I ain't got long to stay here.' "

ON THE following Sabbath, the slaves were all present and eager to learn. A few of the old ones found the studies too difficult. But the young ones learned easily, and some of them were soon reading and writing two- and three-lettered words. Almost as excited as the slaves, Levi made ambitious plans for the future. In addition to reading and writing, he would teach arithmetic and geography.

But the slaveholders thought otherwise.

"We don't like the school," said one.

"Why not?"

"Because when the slaves learn to read they become discontented. I have paid thousands of dollars for my slaves and if they run off I have to send slave-catchers after them, and they're not always successful."

When Levi started to reason with him, he became angry. "If you don't close the school, we'll turn the law on you," he threatened.

"I just hate to stop the school," said Levi to Vestal. "Teaching these people has been one of the great satisfactions of my life."

"We have no choice," replied Vestal. "The law is pretty hard and the slaveholders are scared to death of a revolt."

Levi was still convinced that there was a way to help the slaves, and that one day he would find it. In the meantime, he kept going to his books and ordering more. He also read and reread each issue of the *Greensboro Patriot*.

Some of the headlines in this paper seemed entirely too radical to be true. But Levi wanted to make sure, and so he decided to make a personal investigation.

A nearby plantation belonged to a Baptist preacher. Levi went to his home and asked permission to study the living and working conditions of the slaves. "I've been reading the *Patriot*," he explained, "and I just cannot feel that conditions are that bad."

"Well, in some places they are," said the preacher, "but you can go through my place and see for yourself how I treat my blacks."

The one hundred slaves at this place lived in small, but adequate cabins. Each day those who could work were awakened at dawn and went to the fields under the supervision of a driver at sunrise. Their work continued until 9:00 a.m. At this time they stopped to eat.

"What's for breakfast?" asked Levi, joining a group.

A young man held out a plate filled with mush and sweetened with molasses. "How much do you get to eat each week?" he asked.

"Each of us gets a quart of meal a day — a half a pound of meat and a pint of molasses each week. It ain't much. But it's enough to keep body and soul together I reckon."

After breakfast, the slaves went to work again and continued on until 2:00 p.m. At this time they had their second and last meal, and then they were free to do as they pleased. Some went fishing, others slept, and some of the most ambitious ones cultivated a garden patch the owner had allowed them to use.

From October to March their diet was switched from cornmeal to sweet potatoes and peas.

The slaves on this plantation were allowed to go to church, but they were required to occupy seats reserved for them in the balcony. Their clothes were homemade just as were the clothes of the white folks in the big house. Medical treatment was provided, and none of the adults was ever flogged.

"Well, what do you think?" asked the preacher.

"It appears that you are treating them reasonably well," replied Levi. "They seem to have everything — that is everything except for one important item."

"And what's that?"

"Freedom!"

"Well, that's an item I can't provide. You must remember that I had to pay good money for them. I don't like slavery any more than the Quakers. But this is the way I was raised and so I try to do my best."

Further probing convinced Levi that most slaveholders hated to divide families, and that it was seldom done. But sometimes when an owner fell into financial difficulties, he felt that his only way out was to sell a slave. Quite often husbands and wives were separated and children were sold away from their families.

The plantation the slave feared most was the one owned by the absentee landlord. Often in such situations, the overseer — to earn a bonus — would work the slaves to death, especially if he was raising cotton. In the cotton areas there were peak periods when the work piled up.

Those who bought and sold or worked slaves had a tendency to think of the slaves as subhuman. It was common for an owner — even a religious one — to refer to a sizable number of blacks as a "herd of slaves."

ON A SUNDAY afternoon in the summer, Levi rode Blackie over to Doctor Caldwell's estate and slipped into a slave service that was being conducted by Uncle Frank in a shed. The congregation was singing a spiritual when he entered.

The sight of a white man, however, so dampened the spirit of the slaves, they almost quit singing. Then Uncle Frank raised his hands. "Dere ain't no need for you to quit singin' just 'cause Massa Levi come," he said. "Massa Levi is our friend. It was him and his cousin that wanted to l'arn us to read. Come, now, let's show him how we can sing."

Soon the entire congregation was on its feet. As they sang they clapped their hands to the rhythm of the music. The chorus to the song went like this:

"O Canaan, sweet Canaan,
I am bound for the land of Canaan."

While they sang those words, they looked dreamily at the ceiling as if in great anticipation. Then Uncle Frank started them on another tune in which the words to the chorus were:

Follow the drinkin' gourd!
Follow the drinkin' gourd!
For the old man is a-waitin' to carry
    you to freedom
If you follow the drinkin' gourd.

This song was even more popular than the one about Canaan. Levi scribbled down a verse which said:

When the sun comes back,
    and the first quail calls,
Follow the drinkin' gourd!
For the old man is a-waitin'
For to carry you to freedom
If you follow the drinkin' gourd!

After a short sermon by Uncle Frank, the crowd was dismissed. Then Levi signaled the preacher to stay.

58

"Your sermon was very good," he said. "I think the people liked it too."

"Yes, all slave-niggers would rather hear other slaves preach than to hear even de best white preachers."

"Why?"

"Oh, dat's easy. You see de white preachers always preach de same sermon when dey preach to de slaves."

"And what sermon is that?"

"Well, dere only sermon seems to be from de words of Peter: 'Servants, be subject to your masters with all fear.' My but you should hear dem preach on dat subject! Most of 'em gets so excited dey pounds de pulpit and claw de air as if dey is a-fightin' bees. I's heard such sermons so much I declare I don't want to hear 'em no more nohow!"

"I liked the singing," said Levi. "But don't those words have a secret meaning?"

Uncle Frank looked around cautiously before answering. Then in a near whisper, he confided, "Of course dey do. And all de slaves knows de true meaning' and dat is why dey gets so happy. Dey all wants to go to Canaan — de land of freedom."

"And what's the real meaning of the drinking gourd song?"

"Well you see, it is a-like dis. All de slaves knows dat der freedom is up Norf — 'specially in Canada. And many of de slaves wants to go dere. But how's dey a-gonna do it?"

Here, the old preacher paused and looked carefully around again. Then, arching those great eyebrows, he lowered his voice another notch and said, "De only way for 'em to go is at night when 'de first quail calls.'

59

And, Massa Levi, if you was a slave, and was a-hidin'
in de swamps and couldn't read and de bloodhounds
was on your trail, what would you do?"

"I don't know, Uncle Frank.

"Well de slaves can't read no books and no maps.
But de Lord has put a big map in de sky, and dat
dey can read. Way up dere is a great drinkin' gourd,
and right on top of dat drinkin' gourd is de Norf Star.
So all de slave has to do is to follow de Norf Star
and so if he can keep goin' and escape from de alligators and bloodhounds he sure 'nuff is a-gonna get to
Canada — and freedom."

"Now I understand," nodded Levi. "I was puzzled at
the meaning of the drinkin' gourd. We call it the Big
Dipper."

Uncle Frank started outside and then Levi stopped
him. "You know one of your young men has a marvel-
ous tenor voice — "

"Oh, dat's Sam — de young man wid de top of his
ear chopped off. He wants to marry my daughter. . . ."

"What happened to his ear?"

"Oh he kept runnin' away and so his Massa down in
Alabama cut it off so that he'd 'member not to run
away no more."

Levi changed the subject. "Uncle Frank, a lot of
Friends are moving out West to Indiana. And I've about
decided to go there too. In Indiana maybe I could
build a big house with secret rooms and help those who
are following the drinking gourd get to Canada. What
do you think?"

"What does I think?" His eyes widened and he
laughed and laughed. "What does I think, Massa Levi?

I think de Lord has been a-speakin' to you. Dat's what I thinks." Then raising a heavy eyebrow, he added, "But I don't think you should go alone — "

"What do you mean, Uncle Frank?"

"As I done said, I don't think you should go alone. No, suh! You should take Catherine White with you. Dose Whites are friends of de slaves and dere mighty fine people — all of 'em. But dat Catherine? Well, dat Catherine am somethin' special, dat's what she am!"

A DIFFICULT
DECISION

A THIN, banana moon was riding high as Levi and Katie seated themselves on the swing at the end of his father's veranda. The chirp of a cricket and the dim fragrance of mountain laurel filled the humid, summer air. In the distance, the jagged peaks of the Blue Ridge Mountains were shadows against a blackening sky still aflame with the final rays of the sun.

"Katie," began Levi, holding her slim hand in both of his, "I've wanted to have a serious talk with you for a long time." He gave the swing a shove with his foot. "I've been doing a lot of thinking in the last few weeks — and I don't know what to do. I'm like a man at the fork of a road. I see the signs and yet I don't know which way to take.

"As I've often said, I'm convinced that God wants us — you and me — to fight slavery with all we have. But fighting slavery is an impossible task. Impossible!

It's like dipping out the ocean with a spoon. I've been burning my candles late recently. And the more I read the more overwhelmed I become." He drew her close. "You know how our Methodist and Baptist friends love 'Amazing Grace.' "

"Yes, it's a great hymn. What about it?"

"Well that hymn was written by John Newton — and John Newton was a slaver! And he was one of the worst. He used to cram his ships so full of slaves they could hardly move or even breathe. Then, because of a storm in which he nearly drowned, he became a Christian. Even so, he continued to buy and sell slaves. And it didn't bother his conscience. Not in the least. It was not until he became a preacher that he was convinced •of the vileness of the trade. Look, I have a quote from his own pen."

Levi fished an old envelope from his coat pocket. Holding it close to the light splashing from a row of candles in the living room, he read, "During the time I was engaged in the slave trade I never had the least scruples as to its lawfulness."

"Now what do you think of that?" he demanded.

"I — I really don't know what to say," shuddered Catherine.

"And remember too that Newton was a man of prayer. Yes, he loved to pray. And yet sometimes when he prayed there were hundreds of slaves just beneath his knees. And some of those slaves were nearly suffocating.

"However Newton wasn't the only one who kept a clear conscience about slavery," continued Levi, tapping the envelope on his thumb. He spoke like a defense lawyer summing up a case before a reluctant jury. "Oh, no. There were others. All of us have heard of Richard Baxter — the great Puritan preacher of the last century. Well, he said that those who worked slaves and *neglected their souls* were 'incarnate devils.' That was great, Katie. But he didn't see that it was wrong to own another human being."

Driven from the veranda by the villainous mosquitoes, Levi led the way into the living room. His parents and little sister, Priscilla, were absorbed in their reading when they entered.

"I thought it was about time for you to come in," said Prudence Coffin, a wide smile crossing her round face. "Now, how about some refreshments? I have a pan of fresh cookies and there's a pail of cool milk hanging in the well."

As his mother was setting the table, Levi brought down an armful of books and fanned them out on the desk.

Opening a thick volume, Levi said, "No missionary has influenced me more than John Eliot. He worked himself to death preaching to the Indians. And yet when he wrote about slavery he did not condemn it. Instead, he advised the slaveholders that they should "bring their poor Negroes unto the Lord."

Levi held up the book and pointed to the place where he had underlined the sentence.

"Are you trying to say that the Christian world has failed?" asked the elder Coffin from his place by the grandfather clock.

"Certainly not! The churches have done more than anyone else to abolish all sorts of evil things. What

64

I am saying is that truth takes a long time — a terribly long time — to sink into the human brain and be accepted. None of us honor any human being more than George Fox. He established the Society of Friends and taught the world about the Inner Light. And yet — "

'Don't you criticize George Fox," interrupted Catherine.

"No, Katie, I'm not going to criticize him. I want to point out something. When Fox went to Barbados in 1671 to visit the Friends, he stayed with Friend Lewis Morris. And Friend Lewis Morris owned scores of slaves!

"Later, when Morris died in America and his will was probated, it was learned that he had willed sixty-six slaves to his friends — and some of his friends were Quakers! Moreover, no one, not even a Friend, objected." Levi shook his finger for emphasis.

"But that same year Fox said that slaves should be released — after they had served thirty years. Those thirty years sound terrible to us today, and they will sound worse one hundred years from today. But Fox, you see, was just beginning to see the truth."

Prudence Coffin disappeared into the kitchen. Then she returned with the milk and cookies. "Doctor Caldwell said that Levi would make a good preacher, and I think he was right. Now let's forget about slavery for a while and enjoy these refreshments," she said with a smile.

Levi, Sr., took a bite out of his cookie and then turned to his son. "Something seems to be bothering you. What is it?" he asked.

"It's as I told Catherine. I've come to a fork in the road and don't know which way to turn. A lot of our friends are moving West to Indiana. Maybe I should go with them. Indiana is free.

"On the other hand, how can we teach the people here that slavery is wrong if we leave?"

"But how can you stop slavery all by yourself?" asked his father.

After refilling his glass with milk, Levi replied, "I've been thinking of teaching school and starting a library. Books can change people's thinking. Maybe God wants me to stay here in this darkness and light a candle."

"Did you know that Benjamin White just sold his farm?" asked Catherine eagerly. "He closed the deal today. He says he's going to Indiana."

"And maybe I'll go with him," said Levi. "You know I halfway promised Uncle Frank that I'd build a home in Indiana and let the runaways spend time with me as they try to get to Canada."

"But if you do that you'll be breaking the law," said his father.

"Not necessarily," replied Levi with some animation. "Remember Stephen? We got his freedom and we didn't break the law. And besides the Fugitive Slave Law of 1793 is not respected in every state. What the story is in Indiana I don't know. But I'm going to find out."

"I like your spirit," said his father. "But you must be careful. The Good Book says that we should be as 'wise as serpents and as harmless as doves.'"

"Yes, I know," replied Levi thoughtfully. "That's the reason I want to start out the right way. I feel like I'm starting a furrow. I want to know where to start, and at least approximately where I will end."

"You must follow the Inner Light, said his mother.

"I know all of that," replied Levi, getting to his feet. "But when you go out to shoot a bear you want to be sure that your gun is loaded and that you know what you're doing."

"True," replied his father. "But you can't take on slavery all by yourself."

"Maybe not," said Levi, pacing back and forth. Nevertheless if you're going to accomplish anything you've got to put your heart in it. William Penn and George Fox were willing to go to prison for their faith — and so am I."

"How about you, Catherine? Would you be willing to go to prison for your faith?" asked Prudence Coffin.

Of course!"

"Then that settles the matter," said Levi, Sr. "And maybe now we'd better go to bed. Prudence, get Catherine a candle and show her the way to the guest room."

AS THE seasons changed, Levi continued to study, make notes, and pray for guidance. He read the *Greensboro Patriot* avidly and when Benjamin Lundy started the *Genius of Universal Emancipation,* Levi subscribed at once.

These papers helped originate a number of antislavery societies. Delighted with this move, Levi joined one of them. He was deeply encouraged to learn that a number of slaveholders were halfway interested in manumitting — freeing — their slaves. But this vague desire to free their slaves gradually was coupled with an insistence that all the freed slaves be immediately returned to Africa. This insistence disappointed Levi. He explained his feelings to Catherine. "If the Negroes want to return to Africa, that's fine," he said. "But we have no right to force them to leave this country."

When it was announced that the next convention would be held in General Gray's barn in Randolph County, Levi attended. His hopes were high, for General Gray was a slaveholder and a wealthy man. The new barn had been roofed but it had not yet been boarded up. Since the spring weather was clear, it was an ideal place to meet.

Running his eyes over the crowd, Levi noticed many Friends and a surprisingly large number of slaveholders. These slaveholders, he soon learned, were interested in "gradual manumission." This feeling was expressed quite clearly by a stout, bald man from Greensboro. Standing at the front, his thumbs hanging in his suspenders at the waistline, he said, "The missus and I want to free our slaves. But we paid hard cash for 'em, and so we want to do it gradually. After all, we've got to think about our family — and heirs. We have agreed that we'd be willin' to free 'em after they have earned back for us 'bout what we paid for 'em. And that might take twenty years, or even more. Our money don't grow on trees."

The length of time that the slaves would be required to work before they were freed was argued back and forth. And then the idea that all freed slaves should be immediately returned to Africa was presented.

"Gentleman," said a former sheriff, "I ain't got much education. But I'm a realist. Yes, I believe in gradual manumission. But what's gonna happen to the regular slaves when they see the freed ones shufflin' around doin' nothin'? I'll tell you what will happen. It will make 'em discontent. And gentlemen, I'm speakin' from experience. I've dealt with niggers all my life — and I know the score. A free nigger or two could stir up the slaves all over North Carolina. My advice is that when we free 'em we should ship 'em straight back to Africa!"

This speech was acclaimed by cheers. "That's the truth," agreed one. And another said, "We must never forget what happened in Santo Domingo."

A slender Friend whom Levi did not know now pushed himself up to the podium. "Friends," he said in a firm loud voice, "I think we are forgetting one thing. A good portion of the slaves in this state were born here, just as most of us were born here. And since none of us have to leave the state, I don't think — "

"Yeah, but we're white and they're niggers," interrupted a voice.

"That makes no difference," said the Friend. "God is the Father of all of mankind."

"You Friends make me sick in my stomach!" said the ex-sheriff seizing the podium and elbowing the former speaker out of the way.

With a deft movement of his tongue, he transferred a huge wad of tobacco from his right cheek to his left. "Have you all plumb forgotten our history?" he demanded, glaring at a knot of Friends in the center of the rough benches. "Don't you know that by 1793 slavery was almost finished in the South? I can still remember them days. Niggers on the street were almost as scarce as mittens on an alligator. Then Eli Whitney came down to Georgia and in ten days or so he invented the cotton gin.

"With this new invention a man could prepare fifty pounds of cotton in a day — and England wanted all the cotton we could produce. And so what did we do? We busted our sides plantin' cotton. You bet your life we did! And it wasn't long until the whole country looked like we'd had a snow blizzard. Then we had to buy niggers to gin it. Before Whitney's invention you could buy a good field hand for less than $500. Now a good field hand will fetch $1,200 — and even more. Indeed I saw in a newspaper the other day where a man wanted $500 for a 50-pound boy. Gentlemen, that's $10 a pound. In my book that's a lot of money.

"And so you can see — and it's as plain to me as a hat on a Quaker's head — that if God was really against slavery He wouldn't have allowed that Yankee from Massachusetts to invent his machine!"

He stopped just long enough to squirt a stream of tobacco at a one-eyed cat that was sneaking by. Then with his head confidentally thrown back, and his hands balled into fists, he concluded, "If God hadn't given Whitney his brains, he couldn't have invented the cotton gin. And that proves to me that God approves of slavery. But still, since me and my wife are generous people, we want our slaves — all of 'em — to be free. Of course, before we turn 'em loose we want our money back. Every cent. Plus interest and the money we've been out to feed and clothe 'em. Then after

70

we've freed 'em, as I said, we're all for shippin' 'em back to Africa."

Illogical arguments like this continued for over an hour. Then a motion was made and seconded that the name of the organization should be changed to "Manumission and Colonization Society."

"I'm not for colonization," said Levi. "I think the best plan is to free the slaves and then hire them for wages or let them go to a free territory. The Negroes have rights just as the whites have rights. None of us have a right to dictate where they should live!"

It was a brave speech. But no one — not even a Friend — supported Levi. When the question was called for, it carried by seven votes.

At the end of the meeting a Friend with a double chin slapped Levi on the back. "I agree with the stand you took," he said, "and I voted against the motion. I think all of the Friends had better withdraw from the society and form their own."

Levi thought of asking why he had not supported him with a speech. But he thought better of it, and was silent. Nevertheless, a speech or two might have defeated the motion. The silence of his friends — especially the Quakers — was hard to accept.

BENJAMIN WHITE was waiting for him when Levi returned home. "We're leaving for Indiana on Fourth Day!" he said, shaking his hand. "We've had all the slavery that we can stand, and I can hardly wait to get started. The whole family's going — all six of us. It'll be a rough trip. Since you're pretty good with horses, we'd like you to drive the team."

71

"How long will it take?"

"Oh, a month to six weeks."

"That's a long time."

"Yes, but it's a long trip — around six hundred miles." Ben pulled out a rough map and unfolded it on the table. "This is the best way to go," he said, tracing the route with his finger. "We'll cross the Blue Ridge Mountains at Ward's Gap in western Virginia. Then we'll cross Tennessee and Kentucky."

"And where will you cross the Ohio River?"

"At Cincinnati. And Cincinnati is only a four or five days' journey from the place where we're moving on the White Lick in southern Indiana."

"I've been sort of expecting and hoping that you'd ask me," confessed Levi. "But since it's a major trip and since Priscilla would be the only one of the children left at home I'd better talk it over with the folks. They're getting up in years. I'll let you know on First Day."

"Well if you decide to go, you'd better bring a good gun and plenty of powder. We'll be living in a tent and it would be nice if we could kill some game and catch a few fish on the way."

After Levi had gone to bed that night, he found the latest copy of the *Patriot* folded up next to his candle. The lead story this time concerned a slave-catcher who had cornered his victim with some bloodhounds just as he was about to cross the Ohio River. The chase had been so long the catcher was angry and took out his spite by chopping off part of the man's right foot with an ax.

The slave almost bled to death.

"And the pity of this tragedy," editorialized the writer, "is that the perpetrator of this unnecessary and brutal tragedy will never be punished. And if there were a law that would condemn him, it could not be used, for a slave is not allowed to testify in court! It is about time the churches woke up and took a stand against this open sore that is slowly but surely draining away the vigor of the South."

Before blowing out the candle, Levi knelt by his bed and prayed for guidance. "Lord, show me how to help and lead me to the right place," he pleaded.

INDIANA AND THE
SLAVE-CATCHERS

ORIGINALLY, Ben White and his wife — Levi's sister — and their four children were the only ones scheduled for the trip. Then Ben's niece had begged to go along. Now there were eight in the party.

There was a lump in Levi's throat when he kissed his family and Catherine good-bye. "I'll write as soon as we get to a place large enough to have a post office," he managed to say as he snapped the reins.

The days were crisp and bright and everyone in the wagon was excited about what was ahead. Each evening the tent was pitched by the side of the road. Then a roaring campfire was kindled, the food cooked, and their large watchdog chained outside to guard. The tree-drenched mountains, verdant valleys, waterfalls, and rivers along the way were magnificent and Levi managed to shoot several wild turkeys.

After they had been traveling for nearly a week,

two rough-looking men galloped up.

"We've lost our dog," explained one of them, "and we think that he might have crawled into your wagon. And so please let us make a search."

"I can assure you that we don't have an extra dog," said White. "Besides, we're Quakers. All of us. We don't steal."

"Ah, we've heard that kind of guff before!" answered the spokesman, a middle-sized man with a bristling growth of unusually black whiskers. "Just stand by. We won't do no damage!"

"Do you have a warrant?" asked Levi, blocking the way to the wagon step.

"No, we hain't got no warrant, and we ain't officers of the law. We've just lost our dog and, by thunder, we're gonna find him!"

The pair barged into the wagon like greedy thieves. They tumbled everything around and made a terrible racket. Finally they jumped to the ground. "Sorry," said the lips behind the whiskers. "Our mistake."

"What were you *really* looking for?" asked Levi.

"Our dog, just as I said. A man shore hates to lose his dog. Specially when it's a valuable dog like — like Tim."

Levi stepped back into the wagon. Then he hesitated. "Where was that dog?" he asked. "You don't seem to have a wagon, and — "

"We was huntin' rabbits and the dog ran ahead. But say, if you wanna fight we're ready to 'blige! Ain't we, Andy?" He jabbed his companion in the ribs and took a step forward, his fists clenched. "Me and Andy ain't accustomed to takin' no sass from anyone!"

Without bothering to reply, Levi drove on. The northern sky was fringed with dark clouds and the group was anxious to get to Abingdon where they could buy supplies and mail their letters.

A DOZEN dingy posters on the wall of the tiny log post office offered rewards for clues leading to the arrest of several notorious criminals. And hanging by these advertisements were four or five others offering large sums for the apprehension of runaway slaves.

After mailing a letter to his parents and another to Catherine, Levi studied one of the slave posters. He had read such posters before in North Carolina, but this one was so large and gaudy it riveted his attention. The sloppy, uneven printing read:

$600 REWARD!
RAN AWAY from my plantation on the 4th of May, 1822, a family of four slaves.

George is about twenty-two. His wife, Martha, is about nineteen. And with them their baby, Jackson, nearly three. Also, Martha's mother, a very black woman about sixty. She has white hair and is stooped. George and Martha are so white they may pretend they are white. Both are very intelligent and have strong, crooked teeth. George has the letter T branded in his left palm. The baby also is nearly white and has a chin dimple.

I will give the above award to anyone who will bring the entire family to me, or for securing them in any jail. Or I will pay seventy-five dollars for the securing of any one of them — dead or alive.

Bud Taylor
Nashville, Tenn.

A nasal voice at the stamp window caught Levi's attention and turned him around. "Gimme a stamp and an envelope," said a waspy looking man in a yellow, checkered vest.

"Just snagged the Hackson family. Caught the whole bunch this time. Includin' both the gals. Am gonna write to their owner and have him bring the money. Wife has been after me for a new silk dress and those three hundred dollars ought to do it!"

"Aren't you afraid they'll get away?" asked the clerk.

"Not this time. I got 'em all handcuffed and chained together. I even had a bell forged on a ring around Mary's neck. Cost five dollars. But it's worth it. There hain't no use of catchin' a fish and then havin' him git off the hook just before you land him. And I don't mind a little expense now and then. It's all part of the nigger-catchin' business." He grinned widely.

"I caught 'em with my bloodhounds. I — "

He would have continued except that a couple of boys had come in for stamps.

Sick at heart, Levi left the post office. The slave family was chained to a tree outside. "Sir, my wife is ill," said the husband, a black man in his thirties. "If you could get us some water to drink, we'd appreciate it."

From the wagon Levi brought a pitcher and some tin cups. After handing the wife a cup of water, Levi said, "How long has it been since you've had something to eat?"

"Not since yesterday, and we've been walking all the time. Martha and Suzi have had a hard time keeping up. Their leg-irons have just about crippled them."

"Let me get you something to eat," offered Levi.

"There isn't time," said the man. "Mr. Johnstone is going to take us down to the jail just as soon as he's finished in the post office."

Levi, however, paid no attention to this objection. He went to the wagon and returned with a bag of sandwiches made from leftover turkey. "I don't know what kind of food you'll get in jail. But maybe this will help. From what I overheard, you've tried to escape before."

"That's right."

"Why are you so anxious to escape? Isn't your owner good to you?"

"Oh, he's middlin' good. We get plenty to eat and he even trusts me with some of his business. But he's in financial trouble and he was going to sell our girls to a man down in Mississippi. And we don't want to — "

"That's 'nuff out of you!" shouted the slave-catcher, waving a horsewhip. "You just got more l'arnin' than that black hide o' yours can stand." Then he turned to Levi.

"What do you mean, talkin' to my slaves?"

"But they're sick and hungry."

"That ain't your affair." He unlocked the chain that fastened the slaves to the tree. "The jail's jist 'round the corner and the jailer will give 'em plenty to eat. The good Lord knows we have to pay him enough whenever we take him a few niggers to board."

He inspected all the handcuffs and leg-irons and then took the chain that linked them all together. "Come on, niggers, I guess we got to go to jail." He had only gone a few yards when he stopped and faced Levi. "If you Quakers would tend to your thee'n and thou'n and leave the slavin' to others, we'd all be better off!"

As the slaves shuffled down the street, the girls turned and smiled at Levi. Their fine, even teeth framed in their tar-black faces reminded him of piano keys. Levi smiled and waved back. But the girls could not wave because the chain that linked their manacles had been drawn taut by the slave-catcher who was pulling them on the double. So instead of waving, they nodded their heads. It was then that Levi noticed the red ribbons at the end of their pigtails.

Levi stumbled back to the wagon to hide his tears from the curious passersby. Just as he stepped inside, he heard the soft tinkle of a bell. Suddenly his struggles were in vain. He wept like a child, and he was not ashamed of his tears.

After the people had returned and the wagon had been loaded with fresh supplies, Levi snapped the reins. But instead of driving straight on, he turned by the jail. The slave girls were looking out the bars of a basement window. This time when he waved, they waved back and their smiles were as bright as ever.

AT THE beginning of the fifth week, the wagon was ferried across the Ohio River near Cincinnati. "And now we're in a free state," exclaimed Ben White as the ferry was being tied up on the Ohio side. "I feel as Moses must have felt after he'd crossed the Red Sea!"

"But our troubles with slavery aren't over just because we're in a free state," said Levi grimly.

"What do you mean?"

"I mean the Fugitive Slave Law of 1793."

"Yes, but that doesn't apply in Ohio or Indiana."

"I wish you were right, Ben, but I'm afraid you're not. That law applies to every state in the Union and, I'm quoting now, *in the territories northwest or south of the river Ohio.* Ohio and Indiana are northwest of the river! And even if they weren't, they are part of the Union. Ohio became a state twenty years ago in 1802. And Indiana became a state in 1816."

"All right, all right. You're the expert. But what does the law mean to me?"

"It means that if anyone hinders the arrest of a fugitive from justice — and this includes all the slaves, and justice means returning him to his master — he will be subject to a fine of five hundred dollars. Besided that, the money will end up in the hands of the slaveholders. And that might not be the end of it for even after you've paid the money, the slaveholder is allowed to sue you for damages. It's a wicked law!"

"What will happen, then, if I help a slave escape?"

"You'll be in great trouble unless — unless you find a way around the law."

"Are there such ways?"

"I hope so. . . ."

"Hey, quit the gabbin'," shouted the ferryman. "There's a wagon behind."

A few days later, the wagon reached Wayne County in Indiana. Here there was a settlement of Friends — many of them from North Carolina and some of them relatives of Levi Coffin.

Although it was an organized state, Indiana remained

80

a vast wilderness. It was filled with wildlife, scattered Indians, and trees. Roads were few and muddy. Often the wagons had to cut paths through the brush and trees. Indianapolis, already the capital, was a new town. It contained only a few hurriedly built houses and many of these were only shacks. There were no paved streets. Pigs, cows, horses, and all kinds of fowl roamed at will.

At Richmond, Levi turned the reins over to Ben White, who was most anxious to get to the White Lick settlement, where he planned to homestead an eighty-acre tract.

Following a three-week visit with his relatives in the Richmond area, Levi borrowed a horse from a cousin and headed toward the place where the Ben Whites intended to settle. On his way, Levi stopped at Indianapolis.

The courthouse in the capital was under construction as Levi rode up. "It's gonna be a fine building," said an apparent official. "And it's about time we got it built. Indianapolis is destined to be a great city. But so far we haven't even built the state house." He shook his head. "We've already elected a state legislature, but we don't have any place for them to meet. It's as I always said, God made fools and then he made politicians!"

Levi watched the workers for a while and then he drifted over to the newspaper office. "Welcome to our great metropolis," said the editor, handing him a fresh paper just off the press.

"From your accent, I'd say you've come from the South. Well, let me tell you something. Indiana's just a new state, but we've got everything it takes to grow."

Outside, Levi scanned the paper for news — and prices. In the *For Sale* column, a "horse in excellent condition" was listed for $40; and in the *Wanted* column a Tom Jones advertized for rail-splitters. He offered 25¢ a day. Eggs were 5¢ a dozen. A child's coffin was $3, while one large enough for an adult brought $7.

The editorial enthusiastically supported President James Monroe and praised him lavishly for having had "the wisdom and foresight" to purchase Florida from Spain in 1819 for "a mere five million dollars."

Levi stayed with the Ben Whites at the White Lick settlement. It was about twenty miles southwest of Indianapolis at the place where modern Mooresville stands. At breakfast, Ben said across the split-log table, "I told a Friend from Georgia about those men who searched our wagon. Do you know what he said?"

"I can't imagine."

"He said that they also searched his wagon for their lost dog. Only they told him that their dog's name was Jack! In Abingdon he learned that they were slave-catchers."

"That's about what I thought," Levi said, glaring at his bowl of corn bread.

None of the people on the White Lick knew it at this time, but just about a hundred miles to the south of them, and a little to the west, lived a thirteen-year-old boy on Little Pigeon Creek whose life was to affect theirs deeply. At the time, the lad was preparing to help his father and the neighbors build a Primitive Baptist Church for their community. His name was Abraham Lincoln.

The Friends around Richmond insisted that Levi stay with them and teach school for a term. Undecided about what God wanted him to do, he agreed. The tiny schoolhouse stood on a low rise near where Earlham College was later to establish its campus.

Levi enjoyed this work, but with a lot of energy left over, he began to look around for something else to do. Noticing that many of the young people could not attend because they were needed on the farms during the week, he organized a Sabbath school — the first one to be organized in that part of the country.

Classes gathered in the afternoon at the Quaker meetinghouse on First Day. Levi taught courses in Bible and other "elevating subjects."

The school was popular from the start. Baptists, Quakers, Methodists, and the nonchurched attended. Levi looked forward to the classes each week and taught them eagerly. But his heart was in the purple mountains of North Carolina — and with Katie. Each week when he wrote to her, he poured out his loneliness. "I am sure that God wants to use us together in His plans," he wrote again and again.

Along with several Friends, Levi began to prepare for his return. As the day for leaving approached, he could hardly wait. Three days before the departing date, he heard the clink, clank of chains at dawn. He followed the sound to the road. There he saw a long gang of slaves handcuffed and linked together.

"I thought slavery was outlawed in Indiana," said Levi to one of the two white men leading them — a thickset man in his fifties.

"It is," barked the man out of the side of his mouth.

"But these are runaways. They was headin' fer Canada. Me and my partner nipped 'em just in time. They were hidin' with some free niggers in Newport."

Levi watched the gang disappear down the road. As he watched, he wondered if he could not have thought of a way to outwit the slave-catchers. Unconsciously his hands balled into fists.

There was snow in the air when Levi mounted his horse and headed for North Carolina during the Tenth Month of 1823. But even as he left the now-familiar land, he knew instinctively that he would return.

MARRIAGE AND A NEW CAREER

QUAKER fashion, Levi and Catherine sent written notice to the clerk of the Hopewell Monthly Meeting announcing their intentions of being married on the twenty-eighth day of the Tenth Month of 1824.

With no objections forthcoming, two couples were appointed to make certain the marriage was solemnized in the plain, Quaker way.

On the special day, Catherine arrived at the Hopewell Meetinghouse. His heart thumping beneath his black coat, Levi appeared. At the door, Catherine took his arm. The pair walked arm in arm to the front. Here, they seated themselves between their parents. In the stillness that followed, Levi's heart beat so loud he feared it would be heard. Sweat formed in the palms of his hands as he waited. He knew he must not appear too anxious. After what seemed forever, he and Catherine arose. Facing the assembly, they joined hands.

85

Nervously, Levi moistened his lips. Then, half-fearing that his voice might be gone, he began in slow, deliberate tones, "In the presence of the Lord and of this assembly I take thee, Catherine White, to be my wife, promising with divine assistance to be unto thee a loving and faithful husband until death shall separate us."

From the corner of his eye, Levi noticed that a number of guests were silently repeating the affirmation with their lips.

Using similar words, Catherine pledged herself to Levi. Then the couple resumed their seats. A wedding certificate was placed on a table before them. Both Catherine and Levi signed, and for the first time Catherine signed as Catherine Coffin. Then the parents signed, followed by all who had witnessed the occasion.

The certificate was read aloud to the guests by one of the members. A long, happy silence followed the reading while each Friend awaited the movement of the Spirit. This was a time of earnest dedication for Levi and he prayed that if someone spoke they would say something that would nudge him and Katie into their life's work.

Suddenly Elder Jeremiah Brown unfolded his long legs and faced the people. As he slowly combed his lengthy white beard with his thin fingers, he said, "I'm glad to have been spared to witness this weddin'. I've known these young people since they were small, and I've known their parents. Now I believe that God has a special work for Levi and Catherine to do. Let us all urge them that they follow the Inner Light.

Folks, there are difficult days ahead." He lifted a shaky finger to his eye. "I've seen the lightnin'." Then he touched his ear. "I've heard the thunder. Slavery is going to rip the Union like a rotten rag. But just as God stood by George Fox and William Penn, He will stand by Levi and Catherine. And Friends I'm going to pray for them."

Two others spoke in much the same way. Then the service was over.

A reception followed in the White home. Among the few who were absent was Jonathan Greene. When Catherine asked about him, she was told that he had moved to Newport, Indiana.

LEVI AND Katie farmed, and in addition Levi taught school during all of the next year. Levi also started a library for the general public. He ordered many of the books from Philadelphia and paid for them with his own money and with funds he raised in the community. He also started a Sabbath school. Like the one he began in Indiana, it was a success from the first. But the charm and lure of the West was upon him. "We must move to Indiana," he said to Katie.

"But what about the school, and the library, and the Sabbath school?"

"God will send others to take over. He needs us in Indiana. He has an extra-special work for us. I can feel it in my bones."

Katie wasn't so sure. But a year after Levi's parents had migrated to Indiana, she was ready for the move. Early in the Ninth Month of 1826, Levi and Katie along with their one-year-old son, Jesse, were up at dawn.

The wagon had been packed the night before. After farewells, the wagon started out. It had just gone about a mile when both Catherine and Levi heard the faint sound of Negroes singing. Levi slowed the horses and listened. A few minutes later Uncle Frank with several members of his "congregation" stepped from the bush.

"You all can't drive off without a-tellin' us good-bye," exclaimed the old preacher. "Don't you 'member dat I'm de one who told you to marry Miss Catherine?"

"Yes, Uncle Frank, I remember. And it was good advice."

"And do you 'member dat we talked about somethin' else?"

"I remember saying that if runaway slaves ever came to my place in Indiana, I'd help them get to Canada."

"And so you did!" He clapped his hands together and rubbed them in glee. "But me and my friends was plumb scared dat you is so busy you'd forget. You *is* such a busy man."

"No, Uncle Frank, I'll never forget."

"Well, to keep you from a-forgettin', me and my friends have practiced a little song for you to 'member us by." As the other slaves huddled close to the wagon, Levi noticed Sam — the teenager who'd had the top of his ear sliced off.

Uncle Frank sounded the pitch, and then with his eyes toward heaven, he led them. In close harmony, they sang:

I looked over Jordan, and what did I see,
    Comin' for to carry me home?
A band of angels comin' after me
    Comin' for to carry me home.

"Now Massa Levi," said Uncle Frank, arching his great brows, "I told you dat our songs has more'n one meanin'. Member?"

"Of course I remember. And in that song the Jordan could be the Ohio River, and the band of angels are white folks who are willing to help slaves get to Canada and freedom."

"You is right. Now everyone knows dat you has a long trip ahead and so we brought you somethin'." From behind a bush he lifted a heavy gunnysack. "Here is some roastin' ears." He pushed them into the wagon. Then he produced a flat brown box. "Dis box has some apple and punkin pies in it. You can eat 'em on de way."

"It was surely kind of you to go to all of this trouble," said Catherine.

"Oh, it warn't no trouble," beamed Uncle Frank, his white teeth shining. "You must 'member dat you and Levi is 'bout de only friends we slave-niggers has." Suddenly tears were dripping from his eyes and flowing into his beard. "De last thing I wants to say is dis. If I never sees you agin on dis earth, I'll see you over dere where dere ain't no slaves and where de overseers don't lash you across yo' back when you stop to rest."

As Levi drove off, the old preacher was pointing to the sky. And then the group began to sing "Steal Away."

WHEN THE Coffins drove into Newport they were warmly greeted by all of the two- or three-dozen Quaker families of the community. A quick survey indicated that a dry goods store was needed, and so Levi immediately secured a building and brought a wagon-load of supplies from Cincinnati.

On the opening day, Jonathan Greene appeared, hat in hand. "It's certainly great to see you here, Levi," he said. "And I'm going to pray that your stay with us will be a pleasant one. But there is something that I think I should say to you in confidence."

"Yes, tell me," replied Levi, as he applied a feather duster to the oak counter.

"It's about slavery. Now we don't have any slavery in Indiana. But a lot of runaways come sneaking through here on their way to Canada. And — " He paused to adjust his wig. "And I know that you and Katie will be tempted to help them. But a number of us don't think you should. You see we believe — "

"You mean that you, a Quaker, believe in slavery!" exclaimed Levi, his voice rising.

"Well, no — not exactly. But we believe that Paul was serious when he told us in Romans 13 to be 'subject unto the higher powers.' "

The conversation was ended by a man and a half-dozen children who had come in for supplies.

The Friends in Newport had already established a Quarterly Meeting and had built a place of worship — the New Garden Meetinghouse about half a mile from the village. Levi and Catherine united with this group and felt completely at home.

From the opening day the Coffin store kept expanding until eventually Levi had to employ extra help. By the end of the year the store was well established. Levi then started another business — that of butchering hogs. After thirteen years with both businesses thriving, Levi and Katie built a large, two-story, brick house. The new home had a basement, a secret room known only to the Coffins, and a barn.

LATE ONE night, soon after the Coffins had moved into their new home, there was a sharp rap at the door. Leaping out of bed, Levi pulled it open. Shivering in the snow, stood three black people.

"Come in," he said without hesitation.

"Someone said that you'd help us," mumbled the tall one of the group after they'd stepped through the door.

Levi responded by asking Katie to prepare something for them to eat. Then after he had closed all the window curtains, he started a fire in the fireplace.

"Where are you from?" asked Levi.

The two men and the woman — all in their late twenties — exchanged glances, but said nothing.

"Don't be afraid," encouraged Levi. "We'll protect you."

"We've come a long, long way," managed the tall one after the woman had nodded to him.

"Your clothes are only rags. How long have you been on the road?"

"Oh, 'bout three months."

"Three months! And where have you been staying?"

"Sometimes we stayed in de woods, and sometimes in de swamps. Last week we stayed wid a white man after we crossed the Ohio. He was shore a fine man. And he's the one who told us to call on you. His name was Rankin and he was a preacher. We've had a terrible time. Before it was so cold the 'skeeters in de swamps almost ate us up. And once we didn't have nothin' to eat for nearly a month. Dat was when de bloodhounds was on our trail."

He might have said more, but the woman kept frowning at him and shaking her head.

Soon Katie had the kitchen table spread and the plates loaded with thick pieces of meat, mountains of mashed potatoes, and a large helping of beans. They were about to eat when the woman said, "Ain't we'd better say grace?"

The trio had just started to wolf down the food when there was a heavy pounding at the door. "Now they're gonna catch us!" whimpered the woman, covering her face with her hands.

"Now don't be frightened," said Levi. "I'll go see who it is. Maybe it's Doctor Way. If everything's fine I'll let you know, Katie. But if it isn't, I'll keep them talking while you hide the guests."

With his knee braced against the door, Levi cracked it open about an inch. "Yes?" he asked. The two husky men he faced were dressed in expensive overcoats and one of them was armed with a wicked looking rifle. Neither had shaved for a week.

"We want to see you about somethin' that's very important," said the one with the rifle, speaking out the side of his mouth.

Levi glanced at his pocket watch. "It's midnight. Why don't you see me at the store tomorrow at say ten o'clock?"

"We can't wait," said the man, trying to put his foot inside the door.

"If it's that important you can tell me now."

"All right, Mister Coffin. We'll be frank with you. A trio of slaves is on the loose and we want to search your house."

"It's too late to do that now. The baby's asleep."

"We insist. Step out of the way. We're comin' in."

"If you put one foot in this house I'll have you arrested for trespassing! Where's your warrant? The law says that you can't search a house without a warrant."

The two men scowled — first at Levi and then at one another. As they turned to leave, the one with the rifle shouted an unprintable oath. Then he added: "We ain't got no warrant now. But we'll have one in the mornin'. And if we find a nigger in your house you'll be in a right smart amount of trouble!"

SOON THE guests reappeared from their hiding place and finished their meal. While they were eating, Levi said, "I don't think you're in any condition to continue your trip tomorrow. You'd better stay with us for a day or two and let us get you some decent clothes to wear."

"But the men will be here tomorrow with the warrant!" exclaimed Katie.

"Oh, no they won't," returned Levi, the slight trace of a smile on his lips. "The judge will not be in his office tomorrow and the next day is First Day — and no court is open on First Day. And so you see they can rest for tonight and at least two more days. And by the time the men get the warrant I'll think of something. But we'd better make sure that no one knows these people are here. Don't even tell the cat!"

THREATENED
BY
FRIENDS

CATHERINE and Jesse were already in their buggy when Mrs. Tom Luckett pulled up in a squeaky wagon amidst a cloud of dust.

"Sorry to have inconvenienced you," she greeted them, waving her hand, "but I've brought you something." She hoisted a large, brown bundle from the wagon. "Maybe we'd better lock it in your house."

The bundle turned out to be a pile of old clothes and a worn pair of boots with one of the tongues missing. After she had dumped the lot on the table, she looked up at the Coffins and beamed. "I'm sure glad that you and Katie are helping these runaways. Here are some things that I brought over to help them on their way."

"Who said anything about us helping runaways?" demanded Levi.

"Everybody knows that," she gurgled. "You have

94

three fugitives right now. Two of them are men and one is a woman."

"Everybody knows that?" Levi and Catherine exchanged glances.

"Of course!" She smoothed her sugar-scoop and cocked her head to one side. "Everybody in Newport knows exactly what everyone else is doing. There are no secrets here. I learned it from Sally Smith, and Sally Smith learned it from Jonathan Greene, and Jonathan Greene —"

"Never mind," said Levi, pulling out his watch. "We are going to be late to meeting."

"I have one more thing to say," persisted Mrs. Luckett. "I think it would be just wonderful if we could organize a sewing circle so that we could help the fugitives. Poor things!"

AFTER THE services were dismissed, the clerk of the meeting, Carl Anken, approached Levi. "Friend Coffin," he said, "we just made you and Doctor Henry H. Way members of the Meeting for Sufferings. You know what that is. We want you to help us care for the needy, and with all the Friends moving here from the South we have a lot of hardship cases. You will accept, won't you?"

"Certainly. God wants us to help one another. I'm always glad to do my part and so is Katie."

"And there is something else I want to talk to you about," said Carl Anken. "It's a rather delicate subject." He peered at Levi over the top of his gold-rimmed glasses and massaged his silky, red side-whiskers. "I do hope you won't take offence, Friend Levi. It's about slavery —"

"Yes? What about it?"

"All of us, of course, are against slavery. But some of us have different ideas. As you know, many Friends have become Abolitionists. They want to abolish slavery right now. But some of us think that a go-slow policy is best. And so Abolitionists are quite unpopular around here."

"So I gather," said Levi dryly. "And what do you think should happen to the slaves when and if they are freed?"

"If that should happen, and I sincerely hope it does — and soon, I'm for shipping them all back to Africa. Our government could buy a special colony, you know. We brought them here, and it's our duty to send them back. That's the only really decent thing to do."

"Even if they were born in America?"

"Yes, even if they were born in America!"

BY THE time Levi got back to the buggy it was piled high with packages for the runaways. "It's about time you returned," grumbled Catherine. "Jesse and I are about to freeze."

"I'm sorry, Katie, but the clerk and I had some important things to discuss. I'm afraid he's soft on slavery. He's from England and doesn't know what American slavery is really like!" After glancing at the bundles, Levi shook his head. "I guess Mrs. Luckett was right. Everyone in Newport knows about our guests. You'd better make them a big dinner so that I can get them on their way tonight. Those human bloodhounds will have their search warrant tomorrow."

Levi laid the bundles in front of the runaways and

told them to select what they needed. It was then he noticed how ragged they really were. The soles in all their shoes were completely gone. Their clothes were in shreds and, altogether, there were only three buttons on all they wore. Levi also learned that the two men were brothers and that the tall man was married to the woman. The younger man had a girl friend who had already escaped to Canada. "And when I finds her," he said, "we're gonna have a regular weddin'. Yes, sir! There'll be a preacher and it'll all be legal. This jumpin' over a broomstick like my mammy and pappy did jist ain't fur us!"

After the last hot biscuit had disappeared, Catherine stood up. "Now, how about some more biscuits?" she asked, her hand on the dough cutter.

"Thank you very much," mumbled the black woman, her eyes on the checkered tablecloth. "But — but we'd better not."

"Nonsense!" exclaimed Levi. "We want to send you on your way well fed. Katie, make them big this time. Most biscuits are too small these days. One bite: half-moon. Two bites: total eclipse!"

"All right, Levi. I'll make them big." For the next hour Catherine insisted that they keep eating.

"Now I'm gonna help you with them dishes," said the black woman as she tied an apron around her thin waist. "And if you don't mind, may I call you Aunt Katie?"

THE STARS were just beginning to shine when Levi was ready to leave with the wagon. "It's loaded with straw," he said. "And maybe you'd better crawl under it until we get out of town. I'm afraid some of the slave-catchers are still around."

The candles and lanterns of Newport were gleaming as Levi drove through the streets and headed for the forks of the road. This time, he did not hesitate. He had already decided on the route he would take. A half hour out of town, he told his passengers that they could sit up and that there was room for one of them to share his seat.

The younger brother took immediate advantage of the invitation. With his ill-fitting overcoat buttoned high and the collar turned up, he seemed lost in thought. The frozen roads were scarred with ruts and the iron-rimmed wheels kept slipping into them and jerking the wagon from side to side. The night was dark and without the light of the stars Levi would not have been able to follow the narrow road.

Here and there a lonely light gleamed from a house and the twisting smoke ascending from the chimneys was gray and fluffy in the blackness. A rabbit or two scampered across the road and the lonely howl of a wolf in the distance pierced the frosty air.

"Them stars are mighty nice, Massa Coffin," ventured the runaway. He spoke cautiously for he had been trained never to speak to a white man unless the white man first spoke to him. "Me and my brother have been a-followin' 'em for a long time. When I was a-hidin' in the swamps with the skeeters a-bitin' me and the alligators nose'n around I often wondered if God made the Dippin' Gourd 'specially to help the slave-niggers. What do you think, Massa Coffin?"

"I — I — really don't know. But I do know that God

loves you and that He made you for a purpose. A definite purpose. And please! Quit calling yourself a slave-nigger. You are not a nigger. You are a wonderful human being. God made all kinds of people. Some are white, some are black, some are red, and some are yellow. The color of the skin doesn't matter. It's what one does with his life that matters."

"No, Massa Coffin. I'se just a slave-nigger. My massa bought me at an auction at New Orleans. I can't read. I can't write. All I can do is chop cotton and I ain't good at that."

"Nonsense! You can learn to read when you get to Canada."

"Dat's what Lulu said."

"Lulu?"

"My girl friend. She l'arned to read all by herself even though she had to sneak into the barn to do it. You see her massa was against slaves bein' able to read. He say readin' ain't for blacks. And you should see de way she can sew! Her needle goes in and out of a hem like a snake a-slitherin' through the grass. Whenever dere was a weddin' among the white folks, Lulu made the dresses.

"Her massa almost petted her until she l'arned to read. When he found it out, he become as nervous as a long-tailed tomcat in a roomful of rockin' chairs. And den he got mean. Real mean! And that's the reason she took off for Canada."

"You haven't told me your name." Levi placed an affectionate hand on his knee.

"Call me Harry."

The clip-clop, clippety-clop of a running horse cut

them short. Levi put his hands to his ears. Then he snapped, "Under the straw!"

Levi knew it was useless to try to outdistance his pursuer, and so he continued on at the slow pace he had been following since he left Newport. "Whoever it is will be here in practically no time," he advised across his shoulder. "If you stay covered and keep as still as death, we'll have a chance to escape."

Soon the tall man on the horse caught up with the wagon.

"Friend Coffin," he shouted. "I have a message. Stop!"

Levi found himself looking into the face of a young Quaker who worked at the store. "Friend Way sent me to st-stop you," said Johnson, puffing a little for breath. "A patient warned him that slave-catchers are waiting for you at Cabin Creek."

"What shall I do?" asked Levi, alarmed.

"Follow me. I'll show you the way to Long's place. He's hidden slaves before."

It was 3:00 a.m. before Levi had turned the blacks over to the courageous Quaker. "They'll be all right," he promised. "And when the road's clear I'll send them to the next station."

Levi started to leave, and then he stopped. From his pocket he drew a black New Testament. "Harry, I want you to have this," he said.

"But Massa Coffin, I can't read."

"Never mind, Lulu will teach you! And remember you are to have a church wedding. No jumping over a broomstick for you."

"Yes, Massa Coffin. I'll remember!"

100

CABIN CREEK was both a Quaker and a black settlement. Many of the blacks there had been born free, while others had purchased their freedom or had been freed by their masters. The entire community worked together to help the fugitives on their way north. A set of secret signals had been agreed to and worked with amazing efficiency.

One afternoon two fugitive slave girls from the South slipped into the home of their grandmother on the outskirts of Cabin Creek. The girls felt that they were safe; but one way or another their owner, who happened to be in Richmond on a cattle-buying expedition, learned of their whereabouts. Since the market price of the girls was about one thousand dollars each, he was determined that nothing would stop him from capturing them. Armed with a warrant, he hired a band of toughs in Richmond to help him.

When the news reached Cabin Creek a teenager sprang on a horse to spread the alarm. As he circled the village, a slave-catcher shot at him. The ball grazed his arm. But instead of frightening him, the flesh-wound merely increased his determination to arouse more people.

By the time the hunters got to the cabin where the girls were hiding, a crowd of nearly two hundred had assembled. Since she was alone with the girls, the grandmother went to the door with a corn cutter.

"If anyone tries to come through this door, I'll cut 'em in two!" she threatened. And to prove that she meant what she said, she swished the blade through the air a couple of times.

Attracted by the commotion, an uncle of the girls

went to the door and demanded to see the warrant. He read it again and again. Then he began to pick flaws with it.

"This isn't a legal search warrant," he frowned. "No one has a right to enter this house." And thus he continued, wasting as much time as possible. He quarreled with every word and every comma.

In the meantime, the grandmother allowed a few blacks to go in and out the door. Unknown to the slave-catchers, some boys' clothes were smuggled inside.

While the uncle fussed at the door, the girls dressed as boys. Then, with slouch hats pulled low on their heads, they crept out the back door. And there, screened from the front by a row of trees, waited a couple of fresh horses, together with a pair of slim riders. The girls were soon mounted and on their way toward Newport. The grandmother waited until she knew they were at a safe distance, and then she allowed the hunters inside.

Those on the outside, waited thinking they would hear screams as the girls were bound. Instead, they heard a series of purple oaths. The crowd began to laugh.

"Maybe they fell in a hole," suggested a bystander to the frustrated owner.

"Or maybe they just flew away," suggested another.

BY THE TIME the girls had ridden the twenty miles to Coffin's house, they were utterly exhausted. The hunters had divided into several groups to cover every road and search every community.

102

"They'll be here to search our house," said Levi. "We'll have to be extra careful."

"Then I know what to do," said Katie grimly. "Girls, follow me." She led them upstairs, and after they had changed their clothes, put them between the mattress and the feather tick.

"That'll keep them out of sight," she said.

"If the hunters show up," said Levi, as he descended the stairs, "ring the dinner bell and I'll be over."

The girls, however, could not keep still. They giggled until the bed shook.

"If you don't stop giggling," warned Katie, "you'll be caught."

"But Missis," rumbled a muffled voice from beneath the tick, "you should have seed ol' Granny wid dat corn-cutter! Standin' dere in her best calico dress, her eyes a-spittin' fire, she looked more like General Jackson den a little ol' granny. It was de funniest thing I ever seed. 'Deed it was!"

Unable to quiet the pair, Katie had to separate them.

The catchers came to Newport, but none had the courage to call on Levi. After several weeks, the girls were taken at night by wagon to Greenville, Ohio. From there they were smuggled to Sandusky and placed on a ship bound for Canada.

JONATHAN GREENE was visibly disturbed as he faced Levi and Katie in their living room. "Ever since you've been here you've made it a point to help runaways get to Canada," he said. "I wouldn't be surprised but what as many as fifty blacks have been sheltered in your house."

"You're wrong, Friend Greene," replied Levi. "I've kept a record, and so far one hundred and seven have gone through our place. And, I understand, more are on the way."

"Don't you know it's against the law to harbor fugitives?"

"Whose law would you rather follow, that of God, or that of man?"

"What does Romans 13 mean?"

"I'll answer that by asking you what Moses meant when he wrote, 'Thou shalt not deliver unto his master the servant which is escaped from his master unto thee'?"

"Friend Levi, you make me tired." Jonathan adjusted his wig which had scooted toward his right eye. "Don't you know that some of these fugitives may be criminals? You may have helped a man escape who had slit the master's throat!"

"True. But, Friend Jonathan, when the Good Samaritan found the man on the road who had been beaten by robbers, do you think he first questioned him to see whether or not he was a criminal?"

"I — I d-don't know. I — I c-can't remember."

"Why don't you go home and look it up? Maybe that parable will ease your mind."

Greene's face suddenly began to puff. His eyes became flames and his normally thin cheeks resembled slabs of raw beef. "I didn't come to argue," he said. "I came to give you a message. You ·and Katie have prospered since you've been here, and you've prospered because the Friends in the community have done business with you. But this won't last.

"Some of us have gotten together and we've agreed that if you don't stop helping the runaways we're going to take our business elsewhere — even if we have to drive miles out of the way!"

He stood to leave.

"Don't go just yet," said Levi, his voice as calm as a glass of cool buttermilk. "Please stay with us and have a piece of apple pie. Katie just baked some this morning."

Friend Jonathan Greene, however, didn't seem to hear.

UNDER THE HAMMER

FUGITIVES continued to be forwarded to Newport from stations north of the Ohio, and the Coffins continued to harbor and send them on toward Canada. Mrs. Tom Luckett organized a sewing circle that kept needles flashing as they provided clothing for the runaways.

A system of alarms had been worked out. Friends in Richmond kept alert for news of slave-catchers. And vital information was immediately forwarded to the Coffins by horseback. The whole process had become exciting routine. But even as the blacks streamed through the Coffin house, a large section of the community — including a number of Quakers — boycotted the store.

There were days when only two or three customers entered the little brick building on the corner. And often they only came for trifles. During one entire day the only sales were two thimbles, a long bar of soap, and a medium spool of black thread. "We don't want to get mixed up with the law," explained those who stayed away.

On one of the most disheartening days, Jonathan Greene stepped briskly into the store. His hands behind his back, he paced up and down and around the aisles like an inspector taking inventory. Finally he stopped in front of Levi who was working on his books near the cashbox.

"How's business?" he asked, his arms akimbo.

"It could be better, Friend Jonathan," replied Levi, forcing a smile.

"I'm sorry to hear that. I was in business once myself, and I know what it's like to go broke. But, Friend Levi, there is no need for you to go broke. You have a good location. Your prices are reasonable. And you treat your customers well. The only problem is that you persist in helping these runaways. Now if you would — "

"Katie and I have made up our minds, Jonathan. And if you don't like what we're doing, I'm sorry. God will see us through. Good day!"

"But Friend Levi — "

"I said good day!" Levi snapped his book shut and held out his hand.

"THINGS are getting tough, Katie," said Levi after flopping into his rocker. "The store business has gone to nothing and we have a note that will be coming due in the State Bank in Richmond. And all of this is because we're helping the slaves. Jonathan Greene came in today, and you should have heard him. He's

107

the one who's stirred up the whole mess."

"Well, should we close our doors to the slaves?"

"Never! I'm convinced that we're doing right — and that God is pleased. But whenever a new idea comes into the world, it is always accompanied by pain."

"But how are we going to pay the note?"

"That's one of the things I want to discuss with you. I've decided to take some horses to North Carolina to sell, and several other people want me to take theirs along as well. We should make a good profit, and that will pay the note and tide us over. But I'm afraid you'll have to keep an eye on the store and take care of the fugitives."

THE HORSES sold well and by the time Levi reached New Garden in North Carolina, they were almost gone. Better still, he had made a sizable profit. He remained at New Garden, visited old friends, said hello to Uncle Frank, and then continued on to South Carolina where he expected to sell the last of the drove.

In one of the smaller towns, he noticed a big crowd milling around the courthouse. Thinking that this would be an ideal place to dispose of his horses, he tied them up by a restaurant and pushed his way through the throng.

To his surprise, he found that he was watching a slave auction. A high wooden platform with ascending stairs had been placed near the courthouse steps. On this platform stood the auctioneer, hammer in hand.

A knot of slaves who were to be sold stood at the base of the stand. Each slave was handcuffed. Soon Levi noticed some prospective buyers examining the slaves.

108

"Let me see your teeth," said a clean-shaven white man to a jet-black slave.

The slave opened his mouth and the man peered inside. "I'll be dogged if I'll buy a nigger with bad teeth," he said. "A nigger with a toothache ain't much good.

Apparently satisfied with his teeth, the man asked him to jump up and down while he watched his reflexes. Then he noticed a series of six-inch scars on the slave's back. "How did you get 'em?" he asked.

"An overseer whopped me with a rake," mumbled the slave.

"So you're a lazy critter!" sneered the would-be buyer. He thoughtfully aimed a stream of tobacco juice at a bottle and hit it dead center. "I don't know whether I can afford to buy a lazy bastard or not. Choppin' cotton in the hot sun ain't easy. But let me see your muscles. That's right, flex your muscles."

He touched the man's biceps and scratched his head as he considered the limit on his bidding.

After several plantation owners had examined this slave, the auctioneer led him by a chain to the platform. "Sam's a mighty nice slave," said the auctioneer in a singsong voice. He pointed to his broad shoulders with the handle of his mallet. "Has good teeth. Can shoe a horse. Is popular with the wimmin. And has never run away. What am I bid?"

The bidding started at $500 and he was finally sold for $850. "That was a right reasonable price," muttered a man next to Levi. "But I was a-feared to bid. He didn't have much wind and them scars on his back looked pretty fresh. Some niggers never learn!"

As each slave was led to the block, Levi noticed the

way the victim searched the crowd. Apparently each one hoped he would be sold to a kind owner.

Soon a ten-year-old with light skin, semi-kinky hair, and large expressive eyes, was facing the buyers.

"He's a real buy," said the man with the hammer. "Willie is a hard worker. He's been workin' since he was six. Smart buyers buy 'em young and l'arn 'em to do whatever they want 'em to do. This boy would look mighty sharp on a coach. Or he'd make a first-class waiter. Dressed in livery, he'd add a touch to any man's house. Come. What am I bid?"

"How 'bout sellin' him with his ma and sister?" asked a voice in the crowd.

"Sounds good," said the auctioneer. "But maybe some of you gentlemen would like to examine the mother and the little gal first. And while your doin' that I'll have a drink."

Soon a number of men were walking around Willie's mother and sister. The finely sculptured woman was in her middle thirties and her daughter was perhaps six. As the men observed her from every angle, one or two made obscene remarks to which the crowd responded with a roar of barnyard laughter.

"Now this ain't no place for dirty talk," said the auctioneer. "And so let's get busy." He motioned for the woman and her daughter to stand by the side of Willie. "Now what am I offered for the entire family?"

"A thousand dollars," boomed a voice.

"Now listen, gentlemen," said the auctioneer, "this woman ain't no ordinary slave. She's a good cook, a good seamstress, and she's a good Christian. And that means she don't steal."

"If she's a camp-meetin' Christian I wouldn't want her," sneered a man in the front.

"Why not?" asked the man next to him.

"Because — because she'd shout too much, and because — "

"And because she wouldn't let you have children by her to sell at auction!" finished the neighbor. A wave of coarse laughter followed the remark, for its truth was painfully apparent.

Since no one wanted the entire family, Willie was sold alone for $650, and his sister was bid in for a mere $300.

Suddenly the black woman was sobbing. "My children are all gone and I'll be alone," she wailed. "Yesterday you sold my twins and now you've sold Willie and little Ruthie!" Catching the eye of the man who had purchased Willie, she pleaded, "Please buy me. Please!"

"I can't. I hain't got no more money."

Soon the man who had bought Ruthie stepped forward to take the little girl. As he did so, the woman looked deep into his face. "Why don't you buy me so that I can live with my baby?" she begged.

When the man hesitated slightly, she sank to her knees. "Please, please buy me. I'll work for you night and day. I'll sew your clothes. I'll chop your cotton. I'll work all night."

The man looked her over carefully again. "All right," he said. "I'll bid $700."

"$700 — $700, I'm bid $700. Who'll make it $800?"

"$750."

"$750 once. $750 twice — "

"Oh, please bid more," begged the woman, tears flowing down her cheeks and soaking into her cheap green dress.

The auctioneer waited for the man to raise his bid. Instead, he sauntered away, dragging little Ruthie by the hand.

The mother crumpled to the floor and wept so hysterically her whole body shook. "I'll never see my children again. I'll never see my children again," she sobbed.

The new owner yanked her to her feet. "If you don't shut up I'll order you to a whippin' post!" he threatened. "Children are children, and by the sight of you I think you'll have some more. After all, you're a pretty good lookin' wench." He winked broadly at the auctioneer. "Yeah, I think you'll have some more — and maybe they'll be redheaded!"

All at once Levi Coffin was so sick on his stomach he had to flee from the scene and be by himself. As he untied his horses, a Quaker stepped up. "Well, Friend, what did you think of that?" asked the broadbrimmed man.

"Such sights make me ashamed that I'm white," said Levi fiercely.

SEVENTEEN
FUGITIVES

"I HAVE wonderful news for you, Levi," said Katie. "Five new families have moved to Newport — and they've started to trade with us! And besides, you've been elected a director of the State Bank in Richmond to represent Newport."

"Are you sure?" Levi stared at her with unbelief mapped all over his face.

"Of course, and here's the letter."

As Levi read the document, his lips broke into a smile. "It's the work of the Lord," he said. "This means that from now on I'll be consulted about loans to be made to our community. And do you know what that means? It means that our neighbors will be treating us with a little more respect!" He then related the horrors of the auction, and when he was finished Catherine was in tears.

Soon Levi's business at the store had so improved he

was forced to hire additional help. Then he converted a gristmill and began to manufacture linseed oil. During these years, an average of one hundred fugitives passed through his home annually. Many of the neighbors, and even some of the Friends were askance, but on the whole they gave him little trouble.

Five new children — Henry, Thomas, Anna, Sarah, and Addison — were born during these extremely busy years. Thomas died in his first year and Addison when he was two.

At dawn one morning, just after Catherine had dressed for the chores, there was a familiar series of raps at the door. Flinging it wide, she faced two abolitionists whom she knew. They were both from Union County, Indiana.

"What have you got there?" she asked, peering at the wagons.

"All of Kentucky," grinned one of the men.

"Well, bring all of Kentucky in!"

The commotion alerted Levi. Dressing quickly, he hurried to the living room. "How many do you have?" he asked.

"Seventeen! We had to use two wagons, and it took us most of the night to get here. Two of the men are slightly wounded."

While Katie and the hired girl prepared breakfast for the nineteen unexpected guests, Levi helped the two white men unharness, feed, and water the horses. Then he returned with them to the living room and learned the highlights of the fugitives' story.

The entire group of able-bodied slaves — they varied from black to light mulattoes — was owned by

114

various masters who lived about fifteen miles beyond the Ohio in Kentucky. Meeting secretly for a long time, the slaves had planned their escape with utmost care. One of the slaves was engaged to a light-skinned girl who was owned by another master. But he had managed to get her away from her home plantation.

The group had saved some money and met at a designated place on the Kentucky side of the Ohio. Here, they paid a white man to ferry them across. They landed on the Indiana side about seven miles above Madison just as day was breaking. Hiding in the woods and ravines until it was dark, they proceeded toward the north. Unable to risk the roads, they walked through cornfields. Progress was slow and tedious.

At one place a band of slave-catchers spotted them. But since a high fence separated them from the mounted men, they had time to break into smaller groups and escape. Nevertheless, the pursuers fired at them and two men were wounded — one with a ball and the other with pellets.

The runaways who had agreed to contact each other with a low, secret whistle if they became separated, managed to reassemble and proceed northward as a group. Following several narrow escapes, they found refuge at the Hicklin settlement. Here, two wagons were provided for them. Now in the hands of whites who cared, they ultimately were delivered to Levi Coffin.

After a hearty breakfast, Doctor Way and Doctor Stanton arrived at Levi's invitation. These sympathetic physicians removed the shot from the one fugitive and dressed the wound of the other.

The story of the seventeen fugitives spread through the community and many of the neighbors came in to see them. Altogether, it was estimated that these slaves were worth $17,000 — a large fortune at the time.

Since the slaves were exhausted from their ordeal, the Coffins invited them to remain for two days. While they rested, Mrs. Tom Luckett and the sewing circle outfitted the entire group with new clothes and shoes.

Sending so many runaways north at the same time was risky business. After considerable thought, Levi decided the Mississineway Route was the safest, although not the shortest way for them to get to Canada. The first station on this route was Cabin Creek. Levi arranged for the seventeen to be taken there during the night and left at the home of John Bond.

Shortly after Levi's drivers returned the next day, a messenger galloped up.

"Friend Coffin," he panted, "I-I have an important message for you!" He looked around to make certain no one was listening. Then he whispered, "Aquilla Jones sent me to tell you that fifteen Kentucky slave-catchers are staying at the hotel in Richmond."

Levi scribbled a note and summoned a worker from his store. "Get a fresh horse and take this to John Bond. Don't waste a minute!"

Unfortunately, the seventeen had already left when Bond got the note. But leaping on a horse, he dug in his spurs and went after them. He caught up with the wagons a few miles away. "We'll have to scatter them," he said to the drivers.

While all of this was going on, the slave-catchers employed three guides and divided into three groups. One company headed toward Newport, another toward Hillsboro, and the third toward Williamsburg.

"Search every home," ordered the leader. "Look under every woodpile and stick a fork into every haystack. This place is full of nigger-thieves and we're gonna find 'em! We'll meet at Winchester."

The group that searched Newport, did so two by two. Approaching children they inquired if they had seen any stray horses or cattle. Then, having gained their confidence, they asked if they had seen any fugitive slaves.

Several antiabolitionists in Newport mentioned how they had seen or knew about the seventeen fugitives who had stayed with the Coffins. The hunters, however, did not knock at Levi's door. They were quite certain that he had been warned of their approach. Instead, they demanded entrance at hundreds of homes in nearby communities.

After many days of searching and not finding a clue, the discouraged men headed back toward Richmond. Three miles north of Newport, they stopped at a tavern for refreshments.

"When we find that Levi Coffin," remarked one in front of the manager, "we're gonna shoot him and burn his property. A healthy slave is worth a lot of money, and it ain't right for him to help 'em git loose. What he does is just as bad as stealin'!"

After the gang had gone, the tavern-keeper rushed to Newport and repeated the threats to Levi.

"Such threats don't worry me," laughed Levi Coffin.

117

"Katie and I are following our Inner Light to the best of our ability, and we know that God will protect us. But thanks for the trouble."

The slave-catchers sent a number of men to search in the lake regions. While they awaited their return, they remained in Richmond and continued to make forays — especially in the Quaker settlements.

One evening a group of these determined men announced in Richmond that they were heading for Newport that very night, and that they were going to drag Levi Coffin out into the woods and hang him. "After we've hung him," said one of them, "we're gonna burn him out. And nothin' is gonna stop us. We'll do it even if it costs us ten thousand dollars!"

Again, one who had overheard the threat was terrified. After arming himself with a pair of revolvers, he sped up to Newport on horseback. It was midnight when he thundered at Levi's door.

"Yes?" asked Coffin.

"This time they're going to kill you!" said the man, his eyes wide.

Levi invited him inside and listened to his story. Then in a calm voice he replied, "An old proverb says that barking dogs never bite."

"But, Friend Coffin, they'll be here any minute." The man pulled out his guns and laid them on the table. "I've brought these for your protection."

"Thanks, but I don't need such protection. God is helping us. When you're on God's side you're safe." He glanced at his watch. "It's too late for you to return to Richmond. Why don't you put your horse in my barn and get some rest?"

THE SEVENTEEN slaves continued on their journey by traveling at night. While resting at Adrian, the engaged couple were legally married. Later, the entire group reached Detroit and crossed into Canada without mishap.

Levi Coffin had almost forgotten about the seventeen fugitives when he and several of his neighbors received a summons to appear before the grand jury in Centerville — the county seat. "If they can't scare us out, they're going to use the law," said Levi to Katie after he had read the document. "But I'm not worried."

The tiny courtroom was crowded when Levi Coffin stepped inside. A quick survey indicated that many in the court were his personal friends. But hunched in the jury was Lot Burk, the owner of the hotel where the fifteen Kentucky slave-catchers had stayed.

As Levi swiveled his eyes at Burk, the hotel-owner scowled darkly and shifted his glance.

Bloomfield of Centerville was the jury foreman. Addressing Lot Burk, he said, "I believe you are interested in the Negro question. If you wish to ask Mr. Coffin any questions you may proceed."

A tenseness settled over the court and all eyes focused on Burk. Levi's palms began to sweat. He closed his eyes and prayed.

"Mr. Coffin," began Burk after a nervous cough, "do you understand the statute in regard to the harboring of fugitive slaves?"

"I have read it. But I am not certain that I understand it completely. Could you read it to me?"

After reading the document to the court, Burk leaned forward. "Mr. Coffin, are you aware of any violations of this statute?"

The question deepened the tenseness in the room. "I know of no violations of that statute," replied Levi coolly. "Quite often people stop at my house for a day or two, and some of these people *say* they are slaves. But I have no way of knowing whether or not this is true, for our laws do not presume that such people can tell the truth."

Everyone laughed at this with the exception of Lot Burk. Levi then recalled how he had taken care of the seventeen travelers at one time. "Those people were tired, hungry, destitute. Two of them had been shot by their pursuers who claimed them as slaves. But I had no *legal* evidence that they were indeed slaves."

At this, Burk seemed speechless. Coffin went on, "I read in the Bible when I was a boy that it was right to feed the hungry and clothe the naked, and to minister to those who had fallen among thieves and were wounded. Also, I never noticed that any distinctions were made in the Good Book in regards to the color of one's skin. And because of what I had read, I took care of the fugitives." Then, focusing his eyes on his interrogator, he asked, "Was I right, Friend Burk, to do so?"

When Burk hesitated, Levi pressed his point. "How does your Bible read? Is it not as I have said?"

"Y-yes," he answered meekly, "it reads somehow so."

Soon after this, Levi Coffin was excused, and that was the end of the matter. But Levi was more respected than ever in that section of Indiana.

WHILE AT a board of director's meeting at the State Bank in Richmond, one of the men said, "I see you've been promoted."

120

"Promoted?" frowned Levi.

"Yes, you've been promoted. When those fifteen Kentucky slave-catchers left town, they said that you were the president of the Underground Railroad!"

"That's strange," replied Coffin with a laugh. "I've never heard of the Underground Railroad before. But it's nice to be president of something, and so I guess I'll accept the honor."

Following a business trip to Kentucky, Levi returned with added bounce. As he gathered Katie into his arms, he exclaimed, "Well, I've learned what the Underground Railroad is; and since I'm the president, you are a very distinguished person!"

"And what is the salary?" teased Catherine.

"There is no salary, but the satisfaction is enormous."

"Hurry up, then, and tell me. I can't wait."

"Well, they tell me a slaveholder caught up with his runaway, Tice Davids, at Ripley, Ohio. You know, that's the place where John Rankin is — the preacher who relays so many slaves to us. He was about to grab his slave on the Kentucky side of the river when the man plunged into the water and started to swim across.

"Apparently the master couldn't swim. But he kept his eye on the slave, jumped into a boat, and started after him. As he rowed, he kept the man's bobbing head in view. He'd almost caught up with him when the man reached the other side. But by the time the white man had tied up his boat, the slave disappeared. He searched for several hours before giving up.

"When he got to Kentucky, a friend asked what had happened to Tice, and he answered, 'He must have gone on an underground railroad!' "

"And so the Underground Railroad is the network that helps the runaways get to Canada," said Catherine. "I like that."

"So do I," Levi agreed.

The cooperating homes came to be known as 'stations' or 'depots,' the wagons as 'trains,' the drivers as either 'brakemen' or 'firemen,' and the hosts along the way as 'stationmasters' or 'conductors.'" He wrapped his arms around her again. "And now maybe it would be fitting for the stationmistress to be kissed by the conductor!"

After an affectionate kiss, Levi started for the door.

"Before you leave," said Katie, "I have some bad news. Jonathan Greene has been stirring up more trouble against us, and Mrs. Tom Luckett says that you and Doctor Way may be dropped from the Meeting for Sufferings."

LEVI COFFIN
ON THE
OFFENSIVE

HIS HORSE was breathing hard when Doctor Hiatt slid to the ground in front of Levi Coffin's home and began to pound on the door.

"Don't break it down!" chided Levi, after he'd opened it.

"Levi, we don't have a moment to spare!" half-shouted the fired-up abolitionist. "Ring the school bell. Send out messengers. Let's get the people out!"

"Why?" asked Levi, glancing at his old friend thoughtfully.

"Ring the bell. I'll explain after you've rung the bell. We've got to get people out and have a meeting. Come, jump on your horse and let's get over to the schoolhouse. And hurry!"

After Levi had heaved the rope a dozen times, he said, "Now Doctor Hiatt, please tell me what's ailing you. Do you have a fever?"

"Give me that rope, and I'll tell you." When the bell began to peal again, he said, "As you know, it is perfectly legal for a slaveholder to cross the state of Ohio, Indiana, and Illinois with his slaves." He paused for breath. "But if he locates in one of those states his slaves are automatically free — "

"So?"

"Well, a pair of brothers by the name of Dawes started out from Maryland with their families and a couple of slave girls. Last week as they were passing through Winchester, the wife of Elisha — the oldest brother — got sick. While they were waiting for her to recover, they found a tanyard for sale. Both of these fellows are tanners and so they decided to buy it.

"But they were shrewd enough to know that if they bought the business they would immediately lose their rights to the slaves, for such a purchase would mean that they had "located." And so they told the owner of the business they would buy it after they had sold their slaves in Kentucky. But as smart as they were, they made one mistake. They bought a load of tan-bark and some furniture. And in the eyes of the law, this means that they have located!"

"And so?"

"And so they've lost all legal rights to those slaves."

"Can you prove that they made those purchases?"

"I can. The evidence is right here in my hand!"

"And where are these Dawes brothers and their slaves?"

"They're on their way to Kentucky to sell the girls. And according to my watch, they passed through Newport just a few minutes ago."

124

"What do you propose to do?" asked Coffin, his head cocked to one side.

"We must get a writ and go after them, for since those slaves are free those men are now kidnappers!"

Within minutes, citizens had started to fill the school. And as they came in, Hiatt explained the situation again and again. The moment a quorum was present, Esquire Curtis took charge. As the matter was outlined, it was agreed that an affidavit would have to be drawn, signed, and a writ secured.

"Do we have volunteers to go after the men?" asked Curtis.

There were none.

Coffin suggested several prospects. They refused. Then someone suggested that Levi Coffin should lead the rescue attempt.

"I accept," said Levi and he immediately scribbled an affidavit. Curtis took the document before the ink could dry and prepared a writ. This he placed in the hand of John Hunt, the constable.

The constable then selected ten men to form a posse. "Now go home and get your horses saddled, get your suppers, and be here at 10:00 p.m. sharp," said the officer of the law.

It was raining when the dozen men started out. Coffin and John Hunt led the group. Since the Ohio border was only six miles away, there was some concern that the brothers might escape.

But at midnight the Dawes' wagon was located in the yard of a farmhouse about one hundred yards from the road. The posse surrounded the house and then Levi and Hunt went to the door. After explaining the matter to the owner of the farm, they placed the men under arrest.

As the posse rode back to Newport with the slaveholders, one of the brothers said to Coffin, "If I could find the man who filed that affidavit, I'd put daylight through him!"

Coffin replied, "If it will afford you any satisfaction to see that person, look at me. I am the man. But it is not I that you have to contend with. It is the state of Indiana. The moment you made the contract at Winchester, the girls were free. Now in the sight of the law you are kidnappers. The lightest penalty for this is a five hundred dollar fine and two years in the penitentiary!"

Hearing this, the brothers fell into a long silence. When they did speak, they were far less abusive.

"Tomorrow," said Coffin as they neared Newport, "there will be a preliminary trial before Esquire Curtis and he no doubt will bind you over to appear in court."

The brothers and the slave girls stayed with the Coffins for two days. He was as courteous to them as possible and Catherine provided their meals. At the men's request, Coffin even sent a messenger to Winchester to summon their brother-in-law and some other friends to appear in their defense. At the same time, Coffin engaged a lawyer in Centerville by the name of Abner Haines to present his case against the brothers.

Shortly before the scheduled trial, Haines went over to the Coffin house and laid out the situation before the accused. He explained that legally they were kidnappers, and showed them the result of several simi-

126

lar cases which had been tried in Indiana courts.

Elisha Dawes' face paled as he listened. Following a whispered conference with his brother, he said, "Mr. Coffin, would you promise not to appear against us if we were to give up the girls?"

"I will promise not to appear against you if you will immediately sign emancipation papers in favor of the girls," he said.

The brothers exchanged long glances. Then Elisha said, "Get the papers and we'll sign them!"

Haines drew up the papers on the kitchen table and they were duly signed and deposited with Esquire Curtis. After the matter was completely settled, Elisha approached Coffin.

"How about letting me take the oldest girl home to be a nurse for our baby?" he asked.

"Oh, but — "

"Please! We'll be good to her."

"Why didn't you think of that before? It would have been easy to arrange. But you wanted to sell her. No, I don't think I can agree."

The girls remained with the Coffins for several years and attended the local school.

This episode tended to divide the Quaker community more than ever. Some thought it was great. Others raised their eyebrows and shook their heads. But Levi merely smiled. Letters had started to arrive at his house addressed: Levi Coffin, President of the Underground Railroad. Such mail indicated that his reputation was spreading.

ELIZA HARRIS

IN THE SLAVE section of a small country church in Kentucky, just south of Ripley, Ohio, sat a beautiful quadroon. The finely molded woman was well dressed and in her early twenties.

Impressed, a white visitor inquired, "Who is that woman?"

"Oh, she's a slave," whispered the woman next to her.

"I-I can't believe that —

"Well she is, and she belongs to Mr. ———— "

"I hope he doesn't sell her."

"Oh, he won't. He and his wife think as much of her as they do their own children. A while back a Southern gentleman offered $1,000 for her. And do you know what the owner said?"

"I have no idea."

The woman lowered her head, and guarding her lips with her fan, confided in a low whisper, "That woman is too good to be your wife, and I'll never allow her to become your mistress!"

THE SLAVE woman the visitor inquired about was a household servant who was married to a nearly-white slave named Lewis Clark. Finding slavery utterly intolerable, he had escaped to Canada. Three children had been born to this couple. Two had died, but surviving little Harry was the joy of her life. Both she and her mistress were unusually good to him.

A conscientious Christian, she had heard many a sermon which insisted that slavery was scriptural and that slaves should "obey their masters." She had made up her mind to do just that, even though her husband was in Canada. But then she learned that her master was in financial trouble and that he was going to sell little Harry. This was more than she could bear, and so she decided to escape.

Late one evening after her masters had retired, she fled with her two-year-old asleep in her arms. Her hopes were that when she got to the Ohio River at dawn, she would find that it was still solidly frozen over and that she would be able to cross it on ice.

Sleeping Harry snuggled close as his mother carried him on and on. Eliza knew the road part of the way, but soon she was crossing unfamiliar territory. Then Harry began to wail and would not stop. This would never do, for the whole area was carefully patrolled.

Coming to the creek, she sat on a protruding rock and opened the lunch she had prepared for her child. Harry ate heartily and then tried to get his mother to eat. But even though he attempted to stuff food into

129

her mouth, she refused. There was just enough and none to spare!

Back on the road, she continued north. Occasionally she heard a voice or the rumble of a wagon. At such times she darted into the bushes and remained until the danger had passed. "Now don't cry, Harry," she kept admonishing. "Pretty soon we'll get to the big river — and when we've crossed that we'll be safe. Yes, honey, we'll be safe." She gave him a tight hug. "And then — and then we'll go to Canada and find Daddy!"

The sun was just emerging when she saw the river. And although her legs ached, she began to hurry. "There it is!" she said. Freedom for her and little Harry was just beyond this "Jordan."

But at the bank her heart almost stuttered to a stop. Spring thaws had come early and nowhere could she see a solid stretch of ice reaching across the river. Instead, the ice had broken into great chunks, and these huge melting slabs were grinding and slamming into each other in the turbulent stream.

Heartsick, she looked frantically around. Perhaps if she could find a place to stay for the day, the weather might — just might — get cold enough to freeze the river again. Suddenly her eyes squeezed shut and she prayed, "Dear Lord, show us the right house."

Nearby stood a little shack and almost instinctively she went toward it.

"Please, ma'am," she mumbled to the plump, apple-cheeked woman at the door, "the ferry isn't running and it's cold. Could I come in and keep my little boy warm?"

"Of cour-r-se" replied the woman with a broad slice of heather in her voice. "It's too cold outside for even the devil! Come in and get war-r-m."

If the couple suspected the truth, they didn't reveal it. And when she kept glancing at the window and jumping at every sound, they acted as if they didn't notice.

The lady of the house provided a fine breakfast of hot cereal and insisted that she and little Harry eat as much as possible.

At lunch, her husband — he was slightly drunk — said, "Now I dunno who you are. But if you need help when you get on the other shide, jusht go to the housh on the hill. The man of that housh is a good man. He keeps a light burnin' outside his winder."

As the sun began to blaze in the west, the slave wrapped Harry in her shawl and started out. But when she got to the river, she found it to be in worse condition than it had been in the morning. The chunks of ice were smaller and they were twisting with greater violence. Instead of going down, the temperature had risen.

Shrugging at her luck, she started to return to the shack. But she had only taken a dozen steps when she heard the distinct sound of horses' feet. A terrified glance revealed a pair of armed men bearing down on her!

She thought of hiding. But this was impossible, for the bank was fairly clear. Furthermore, by the men's actions, it was apparent they had seen her.

With her pursuers only a few hundred yards behind, she leaped onto a cake of ice. And then she went to another and another. By midstream she was so tired she rested on an unusually large piece with Harry at her feet. Then she started out again. She jumped, slid, fell, and jumped again. Her shoes were soon gone and her feet bleeding. Once she nearly crushed Harry's head on the ice. Sometimes the ice would give an unexpected lurch and she would be nearly thrown into the water.

Again and again she missed drowning by a miracle. But the Ohio shore seemed a long way off, and she had to keep going. "Oh, God," she pleaded, "give me strength! Give me strength!"

Her strength ebbed. She felt numb all over. It seemed that she could not possibly make it to the next ice floe. And then she saw trees on the Ohio side. The sight increased her energy. And once again she began to jump, slide, fall, and jump again.

All at once her brain began to reel. Dark spots formed in front of her eyes. And then she felt something curiously warm in her hand. "I've got you and you're safe," said a voice. The white man pulled her up the bank. "I've been watchin' you for a long time. You sure have a lot of spunk."

"P-please, s-sir, take me to the g-good m-man," she managed, prying the words from her lips with almost impossible effort.

The man led her along a path for a short distance. Then pointing to a light high on the cliff, he said, "That's the place. That's where the good man lives."

The Rankin home was empty when she stumbled up to the door. But the door was ajar and so she went in and built a fire in the kitchen stove.

She was drying her clothes when two of Rankin's sons approached. "I'm afraid you can't stay tonight," said the older one.

"Why not?" she pleaded, her heart sinking.

"Don't worry," he said quickly. "We'll get you something to eat and some dry clothes and send you on to the next station."

The slave woman and Harry were bone-weary when they climbed into the wagon. It was a rough ride. But knowing that she was really on the Underground Railroad, she felt confident and managed to get several hours of sleep. At dawn, the wagon reached the next station.

"I've got a couple passengers for you," whispered the driver at the door.

"Bring them in, but be careful. There are some slave-catchers around," replied the stationmaster.

Following a heavy breakfast, she was led to a dark, secret room. Here, with Harry in her arms, she fell into a deep sleep. Five days later on a moonlit night, she dismounted at the Coffins.

Catherine listened in dismay as the weary woman told her story. "You've gone through a lot," she said, "and so has Harry. "You must stay with us for a while and get some rest."

"Am I s-safe?" she asked, her large brown eyes nearly wild beneath their long eyelashes.

"You don't need to worry. Levi Coffin is the president of the Underground Railroad and you are as safe as it is possible to be in these terrible times."

That afternoon, Catherine was preparing to iron. "Give me that iron, Aunt Katie," the slave woman said.

133

"No, no. You need your rest."

"I've rested, and you've done so much for me. Please, let me help. This is the kind of work I did for my mistress." She took one of the half-dozen flatirons from the stove and began to iron one of young Jesse's shirts.

As she worked, she told Catherine about slave life in Kentucky. "I almost feel sinful for runnin' off," she confessed. "Mistress was so kind, and I believe she's a true Christian. We often read the Bible together. But, Aunt Katie, I just couldn't think of parting with little Harry. He's such a sensitive child." She picked up another iron, touched her finger to her tongue, and tested its heat. "When you get sold down in Orleans, there's no tellin' what'll happen to you. I've heard a body don't last long in the cotton fields."

The hours and the days rushed by like a bird's shadow. She taught Catherine some Southern recipes, and within hours the home was filled with a tantalizing aroma of fresh cookies and cakes.

"What is your name?" Catherine asked, not having been able to get a satisfactory reply since the woman had arrived.

But the woman refused to respond.

"Then, I'll give you a name," Catherine announced. "From now on we'll call you Eliza Harris!"

Soon more passengers arrived from Kentucky. Levi loaded them on a wagon together with Eliza and Harry. Catherine had seen that same wagon head out the driveway scores of times. But now she could not remain in the house. Rushing outside, she pulled the driver's sleeve and said, "Wait for a moment." Then she took Eliza's hand into both of hers. "We're going to pray for you, daughter," she said. "And I do hope that you find your husband when you get to Canada."

"Oh, I will, Aunt Katie, and when we get settled you must come and visit us."

Catherine watched the wagon as it lurched and grumbled down the graveled road. She stood silently as if rooted to the ground, and then stumbled back toward the house. Her eyes were swimming and it was hard to see.

JONATHAN GREENE started to trade at the store again. His apparent reason was that since the boycott had failed, he could have more influence on the Coffins by handing them alarming news items.

A choice clipping concerned Charles T. Torrey who had studied at Yale and Andover Theological Seminary. After having helped two hundred slaves escape, he was arrested and sentenced to six years of hard labor.

He died in prison.

"The poor misguided man wasted his life," sermonized Greene after he had replaced the clipping in his purse. "He might have been a great preacher!"

"I don't think he wasted his life, Friend Greene," replied Levi, his voice a trifle sharp. "If I remember correctly, Jesus said, 'Whosoever will lose his life for my sake will find it.'"

"Oh, you make me tired," said Greene. "You're as hard to convince as a tadpole! You've got to learn not to quote Scripture out of context!"

"Why don't you come over to our house sometime?" suggested Levi. "I'd like to have a long visit

with you, and maybe we could share an apple pie.
Katie makes wonderful apple pie."

"Maybe I will," replied Greene over his shoulder.
"Yes, maybe I will. But I'm warning you, when I
come I'll be loaded for bear!"

DIVISION!

"I DON'T profess to be unusually holy," said Levi at the breakfast table. "But I can't feel a deep animosity toward those who insult me and give me the cold shoulder."

He thoughtfully buttered a slice of toast. "The reason people feel as they do is because they don't know what slavery is all about! Just yesterday a man came to the store for some nails. After I'd filled his order, he said, 'You know, Mr. Coffin, there are a lot of good laws in the South to protect the slaves.'

"That's true," I replied. "But it's one thing to have the laws in the statute books and it's another thing to have them enforced. And since the poor slave can't defend himself in court, he's about as defenseless as a mouse in a trap."

Levi finished his toast and then buttered another slice. "Here's an ad somebody mailed to me." He with-

137

drew it from his watch pocket and carefully spread it on the table. The ad, printed on cheap newsprint, read:

NOTICE

The undersigned having an excellent pack of HOUNDS, for trailing and catching runaway slaves, informs the public that his prices in future will be as follows for such services:

For each day employed in hunting or trailing . . . . 2 dollars and fifty cents.

For catching slaves . . . . 10 dollars.

For going over ten miles and catching slaves. . . . 20 dollars.

If sent for, the above prices will be exacted in cash. The subscriber resides one and a half miles south of Dadeville, Alabama.

"But even reading such cold-blooded ads can't give us the *real* feeling of slavery. Do you remember the man who came in with the frozen feet?"

"How could I ever forget him?" Catherine replied. "He stayed for three months!"

"He told me that on his plantation there was a rather grim joke about the bloodhounds. The slaves said that when the dogs trailed runaways they bayed: 'Our Father, I've got a heavenly home up yonder, hallelujah, hallelujah.' But when he got treed himself he didn't think it was so funny. He said, 'Mistah Coffin, when dem dere dogs got me up de tree, all I could see was dere big teeth. Dey almost sceered me out o' my black skin!' "

Levi glanced at his watch. "I'm going to start a program to educate the people around here just like we did in North Carolina. And by the time we get through we may have a few more abolitionists!"

138

"I'm with you," said Catherine. "But I hope it does not cause even more division among the Friends."

TOGETHER with Daniel Puckett and some other energetic Friends, Levi raised money to set up an antislavery library. Levi was delegated to get the first supply of books from an antislavery depository in Cincinnati. The books were lent and sometimes even given to the citizens of Newport.

When interest in the books sagged, Levi — often out of his own pocket — bought new books to circulate. Also, special library meetings were called and reviews were given. At first the going was quite slow. And then here and there a reader would become convinced of the wrongness of slavery.

Soon these persons began to organize themselves into antislavery societies, and these societies invited lecturers to speak to them on the problems of slavery. Most of these lecturers stayed with the Coffins.

One of the speakers who stayed with the Coffins was Frederick Douglass — a slave who had purchased his freedom. Douglass was a very eloquent man and was able to move the masses by relating the horrors of slavery which he had seen with his own eyes. Speaking almost perfect English, he was in great demand.

But the slavery element in Indiana was much opposed to him. At his meeting in Richmond, roughs in the audience pelted him with rotten eggs; and at Pendleton the disturbance was even worse. There, M. C. White, Catherine's nephew, had two of his front teeth knocked out with a brickbat.

This opposition served to widen the division in the

community, and soon a group formed and named themselves Anti-Slavery Friends. The Anti-Slavery Convention of Indiana was held at Newport, and as a result feelings on both sides hardened.

"I hate to see this division," groaned Levi. "The Society of Friends has been greatly used of the Lord, and any division will hinder our testimony."

At this time, Henry Clay, who was seeking the Whig nomination to the presidency, appeared in Richmond. Although he was a slaveholder, many Friends went out of their way to entertain him. Also, it was reported that some well-known Friends assured him that they had no sympathy with the abolitionists.

This affair was like ground glass in the eyes of the Anti-Slavery Friends. These Friends remembered that Clay had encouraged the War of 1812 and had used his influence to get the Missouri Compromise passed. This was the bill that admitted Missouri to the Union as a slave state and Maine as a free state.

In addition to this, the Indiana Yearly Meeting dropped Levi Coffin and seven others from the Meeting for Sufferings. At the conclusion of the session, the Anti-Slavery Friends wanted to remain in the meetinghouse to confer on the course of their future. But they were told sternly that they would have to leave. This confrontation caused hard feelings that were hard to forget.

The result of this friction led to almost complete division. The Anti-Slavery Friends set up their own Yearly Meeting at Newport and established five Quarterly Meetings along with twelve Monthly Meetings.

Many of the Friends on both sides of the controversy

were heartbroken over these events.

And in addition to these troubles, Levi was having his own difficulties. For years he had earned a good living selling products in his Newport store that had been manufactured through slave labor. Now this began to bother him. Again and again he discussed the matter with Katie. "I feel uncomfortable every time I sell something that was made by slave labor," he said. Sometime later he found a quotation that really disturbed him.

"Listen to this, Katie," he said just before they retired for the night. "Here is what no other than John Woolman had to say, 'Seeds sown with the tears of a confined, oppressed people — harvests cut down by an overborne, discontented reaper — make bread less sweet to the taste of an honest man than that which is the produce of just reward of such voluntary action as is a proper part of the business of human creatures.'

"Those words are like a knife in my heart. I feel as if I have actually been helping the slaveholders!"

"What are you going to do about it?" asked Katie as she removed her bonnet.

"I-I really don't know. But when God supplies the Inner Light I'll follow its gleams. Yes, I'll follow it even though it strips me of all my possessions!"

A FEW weeks Later, Levi had just finished his supper and was relaxing with the Cincinnati paper when Jonathan Greene appeared at the door. "I came over for some discussion and that apple pie," he said.

"And I'm glad you came, Friend Jonathan," said Levi. "And I see you've brought your Bible with you."

"Well, you know the Bible says that if you have aught against your brother you should go to him," said Jonathan.

"That is so, but before we get into any discussion let's have some apple pie."

Jonathan cut off a generous portion of pie with the side of his fork and started to raise it to his mouth, and then he laid it down. "Friend Levi, I'm brokenhearted about all of this division. And I know it displeases the Lord."

"I'm also brokenhearted," said Levi. "I wish I could do something to heal the wound."

"You can!"

"What?"

"Stop all this antislavery agitation, and stop helping the runaways get to Canada."

"Oh, but the Lord has helped me in my work with the slaves. And as a real Friend I know that you believe that I should follow the Inner Light."

"Yes, I believe that," said Jonathan warmly, "and that's one of the things I want to talk to you about. Friend Levi, you are a mature man. Surely you know that the Inner Light never contradicts God's Word."

"Yes, Friend Jonathan, I believe that."

"Then you just show me one place in the New Testament where Jesus or any of the apostles ever preached against slavery," said Jonathan. He stared at Levi and carefully adjusted his wig.

"There is no such passage, for the New Testament is not a catalog of sins that are to be avoided. Indeed, Jesus never quoted the Ten Commandments. Instead, He said that He had given us a new one. And what is that new commandment, Friend Jonathan?"

"That you love one another."

"Do you think that American slavery follows that commandment? When I was in North Carolina I saw a slave whose master had sliced off the top of his ear because he had run away. Do you think that was Christian love?"

"There are bad apples in every barrel," admitted Jonathan, crimson spots forming on his plump cheeks. "But tell me, Friend Coffin, didn't Paul send the slave Onesimus back to his master, Philemon?"

When Levi hesitated, Jonathan leaned eagerly forward, and almost shouted, "Well, didn't he?"

"Yes, he did," replied Levi calmly. "But what were Paul's instructions to his friend Philemon? They were very definite. Paul said that he should receive him back 'Not now as a servant, but above a servant, a brother beloved.' Does that sound like he was sending him back to a typical American slaveholder?"

"W-well I-I g-guess n-not."

"You see Jesus did not lay down civil legislation except in very broad terms, nor did the apostles. But as the result of Christianity, slavery had almost completely disappeared — at least in the Roman form — by the time of the Reformation. This modern type of slavery didn't start until just a few hundred years ago.

"If you'll wait just a minute I'll get you a book that tells the whole story."

Levi started upstairs to get the book. And then he remembered that he had lent it to Doctor Way. Returning unexpectedly, he was startled to see that Jonathan had removed his wig and was scratching his head — a red, pear-shaped dome as shiny as a doorknob.

"Oh, I'm sorry, Friend Jonathan," gulped Levi.

"That's all right," sputtered Jonathan, his face as pink as a ripe peach. "Sometimes my scalp itches until I can hardly stand it."

Levi smiled. "I think most of the troubles of the world and most of the difficulties in the church are caused because we don't see people as they really are. If we all had the courage to remove our wigs — and masks, things would be different!"

"I believe you're right," replied Jonathan, good-naturedly. He stood to leave. And then he drew an official looking envelope from his inside coat pocket. "This is from the London Yearly Meeting. They are most unhappy about our division over here. They have prepared a document and they are sending it with a committee which will attend our Yearly Meeting in the tenth month."

"Ah, that's interesting. And who are the members of the committee?"

"William Forster, Josiah Forster, George Stacy, and John Allen."

"Those are mighty fine men," said Levi. "But did you know that the Anti-Slavery Yearly Meeting will be in session at the same time? Ours will be in Newport."

"That's a pity. We are all brethren and yet we will be having two rival Yearly Meetings at the same time and within nine miles of each other!"

"Do you think the committee might visit our meeting?" asked Levi.

"I hope so. But I doubt it."

144

That night Levi Coffin was so troubled about the division he could not sleep.

While working on his books the next afternoon, Levi said, "Katie, let's make it a point to pray that this London Committee will help us all get together again. You know Jesus said, 'Again I say unto you, That if two of you shall agree on earth as touching any thing that they shall ask, it shall be done for them by my Father which is in heaven.' "

As the months wore by, scores of slaves continued to pass through the Coffin house, and Levi and Catherine continued to pray that the division in the Society of Friends would be healed.

THE LONDON Committee arrived and attended the Yearly Meeting in Richmond. But they politely refused to attend the one in Newport. "Since they don't have the slavery problem in England, they don't understand our difficulties," explained Levi to a Friend.

A group of fourteen Anti-Slavery Friends prepared a letter addressed to the committee. Levi, along with two others, was asked to take it to the distinguished men from London. This letter outlined a definite course of action.

The committee received Levi and his companions. But it was obvious that the visitors had already made up their minds on a procedure which the Anti-Slavery Friends felt would be disastrous. Levi pleaded with them, but it seemed that his words were being wasted.

"We have this letter from the London Yearly Meeting," explained one of the four. He touched the bulge in his coat pocket. "It is our intention to visit every Anti-Slavery group and read it to them."

"And if you do that," sighed Levi, "you will ruin everything!"

The committee, however, was determined. They went from group to group and read their document to each one. On almost every occasion, the listeners were not only dismayed but deeply hurt.

Tears were in Levi's eyes as he faced Catherine. "The Roman soldiers who gambled at the cross were decent enough not to tear apart the seamless robe of Christ. But slavery is doing just that to us — the body of Christ."

"We agreed together in prayer that God would use this committee for good," said Katie. "Maybe — maybe a miracle will yet take place."

"I doubt it," replied Levi, almost angrily. "The committee will be in town tomorrow, but they will be staying with William Hobbs — and Hobbs is with the Richmond group!"

"Has God ever let you down?"

"No. But sometimes He works in mysterious ways."

Three days before the committee was to leave for London, the gentlemen came to Newport to meet with the Anti-Slavery group. Levi went to the meeting and listened carefully to what they had to say. But as he listened, his heart sank lower and lower. He had the same kind of hollow feeling in his stomach he had had when as a boy he had faced Doctor Caldwell. He believed the visitors were kind and generous men, still it seemed obvious that they had only heard one side of the story. They were as warped as a green piece of timber left in the hot sun for a month.

Suddenly, Levi felt inspired to ask the committee to come home with him to eat. Katie was always prepared with food for the runaways and he felt confident that she could stir up something tasty for these men. But with their biased opinions, would they come?

When the last document had been read, everyone began to shake hands. Levi worked his way up to the committee. "Please," he said, "why don't you come home with me for dinner?"

"Oh, but we can't," replied the leader. "We've already promised to dine with William Hobbs."

"I have something I'd like you to see," pleaded Levi.

"All right, we'll come," said William Forster, taking him by the right arm. George Stacy took the other arm and the remaining two followed.

After seating the committee in his parlor, Levi excused himself and went into a back room where the fourteen fugitive slaves who had arrived the night before were waiting. Among the group was an aged white-haired grandmother with several of her children and grandchildren. One of the girls had a three-month-old baby. "I want you to follow me," he said, "for there are some gentlemen in the parlor from overseas. There isn't any slavery in their country, but I know that they are friends of the slaves and so you don't need to worry."

Levi stood the slaves in a semicircle and introduced them. Then he took the baby in his arms. "See this innocent child who was born a slave," he said. He handed the infant to George Stacy. Stacy spoke gently to the child and smiled.

Facing the stooped grandmother, William Forster said, "It's a long road to Canada. Do you think you'll really get there?"

"De Lord has been with us dis far," she replied in firm tones, "an' I trust He will go with us to de end of de journey."

"But you are old and feeble," pressed Forster.

"Yes, Massa, but I'se been a-prayin' de good Lord a great while to let me breathe one mouthful of free air before I died, and bress His great name, He opened de way so dat we got off safe and He has guided us to dis good man's house, and he and his good wife has give us clothes to make us warm, and when we rest a little so we can stand more night travel, he says he will send us on. May de Lord bress him! You see, gent'men, dat de Lord is good to us."

After the slaves had returned to the back room, Levi said, "For pleading the cause of innocent babies like the one you just held in your arms, and sheltering fugitives, such as you have just seen, we have been censored. Now, my dear friends, if you fully understood the difference of sentiment that exists, and the course pursued by some of the leading members of the Indiana Yearly Meeting, which led to our separation, you could not advise the ending of our organization, while they persist in their course toward us. Your efforts have strengthened the opposition to our labors."

It was a tough speech, but Levi spoke with tenderness. As he shook hands with the committee before they left, he knew he had reached their hearts.

After the men had gone, Catherine said, "You see, Levi, the Lord heard and answered our prayer. I have

148

an inner witness that today we saw the beginning of the end of the division."

"I hope so," replied Levi thoughtfully.

FREE LABOR

EVERY time Levi took inventory of the goods on his shelves, he did so with a sickening feeling. Each bolt of cloth, each spool of thread, and each sack of sugar that came from the South seemed to point an accusing finger. Produced by the sweat of innumerable slaves, these things were making him prosperous.

For weeks now his conscience had churned and festered over this problem. And then he found a paragraph by Charles Stuart that battered him into action. That paragraph read:

> Their bodies are stolen, their liberty, their right to their wives and children, their right to cultivate their minds and to worship God as they please, their reputation, hope, all virtuous motives, are taken away by a legalized system of the most merciless and consummate iniquity. Such is the expense at which articles produced by slave labor are at-

tained. They are always heavy with groans and often wet with blood of the guiltless and suffering poor.

Levi was so shaken by the last sentence he underlined it and showed it to Katie.

"What are you going to do about it?" she asked, peering at him from over the top of her gold-rims.

"I guess we'll just have to buy our supplies from other sources. But when we do that we'll have to pay more. The competition will ruin us. It seems that we're caught between the devil and a hard place."

"What does your conscience say?"

"Oh, Katie, you shouldn't ask me that! My conscience tells me that I should have nothing to do with things produced by slave labor."

"Then that's the end of the matter."

"Yes, that's the end of the matter," confirmed Levi, his mind made up.

IN PHILADELPHIA, Levi met some prominent Friends who felt exactly as he did. In order to have cotton goods that were produced by free labor, they had erected their own factory. They purchased their raw materials from cotton plantations operated by Friends in North Carolina.

Levi carefully examined several bolts of cloth produced in this fashion. "How much do you get for it?" he asked. When the price was mentioned, he winced. "That will almost ruin my profit margin!" he exclaimed.

"We can't compete with slave labor," shrugged the manager.

Levi bit his lip as he pondered. Across the years he

had spent great sums of money in helping the slaves. He needed every cent he could earn to keep this work going. He argued the pros and cons back and forth in his mind. A vision of his financial ruin appeared before him. Then, Quaker-fashion, he shut out the world and prayed for guidance. A minute later, he picked up a pen, wrote out a large order, and signed his name with a flourish.

From Philadelphia he went to New York City. There, he found a supply house that dealt in free-labor products that were produced in the West Indies, England, and elsewhere. From them he purchased sugar, molasses, indigo, coffee, and other items.

With these orders on the way, Levi Coffin returned to Newport with a clear conscience and a quickened step. "Our income may be cut in half," he confided to Katie, "but that's all right. I'd rather be poor and have a clear conscience than rich and know I was doing wrong!"

Levi tried not to raise the prices in his store. This, however, was impossible, and the increased prices hindered business. "I like to trade with you, Levi," said an old man with a bald head and snowy side-whiskers. "But wife and me don't have an awful lot of money. We have to watch our pennies." Then in a confidential tone, he asked, "Do you really think it makes all that difference? After all, Levi, you're just one person. If you quit buyin' slave-produced products it ain't gonna make much difference to the slaveholders, now is it?"

"No, it won't make much difference to the slaveholders," agreed Levi. "But it will to me and I have to look at myself in the mirror every morning."

"Maybe you're right," said the man. "Anyway, if you don't see us around, it ain't because we're mad at you. It's just because we have to watch our pennies."

Levi tried to appear cheerful, but it was hard. This old man was one of his best customers. Indeed, he had continued to shop with him during the entire period of the boycott. Losing him was like losing a son.

The abolitionists and Anti-Slavery Friends continued to shop with Levi even though they had to pay slightly higher prices. But even some of these supporters weakened when they happened to be in Richmond or other neighboring towns. At such times they smothered their consciences and loaded their wagons at the lower prices.

By the end of the first quarter, the profits of the store were down nearly 70 percent.

"If it keeps on like this we're going to go broke," groaned Levi after he had thumped his books shut. "Maybe we should have compromised with our principles."

"And suffer a guilty conscience?" asked Katie.

Levi got up and paced around. He glanced in the mirror and then went over to Katie. "No, I guess you're right," he said. "I'm sure God will take care of us and supply the funds to take care of the slaves."

GRADUALLY the idea of shunning slave-produced goods spread throughout Indiana and the neighboring states. Dozens of communities began to patronize such places of business. By 1846 there were so many free-labor stores a convention was held at the Salem

Friends' Meetinghouse a few miles southeast of Liberty, Indiana. At the end of a crowded two-day meeting it was decided to establish a wholesale depot in Cincinnati. This store would supply the free-labor stores over a wide area.

Three thousand dollars were raised to finance the venture and Levi was invited to become the manager.

"But I can't do that," he protested. "I've lived in Newport for twenty years!"

The free-labor people, however, would not give up. Week after week Levi received insistent letters from them encouraging him to move to Cincinnati.

"And who will look after the slaves if we move?" asked Katie.

"Oh, there are many that would do that." Levi began to count them off on his fingers. "There's Doctor Way, Daniel Huff, William Hough, Daniel Puckett, Thomas Edgerton, Samuel Nixon — and at least a dozen others. The library work has convinced a lot of people."

"But, Levi, you are already forty-nine! Aren't you afraid to make such a drastic change?"

"No, Katie, I'm not. I already know a lot of people in Cincinnati and it won't take long to make new friends."

Soon, those who wanted him to take charge of the wholesale depot came up with a new tactic. They suggested that he take the position for a "mere" five years. This suggestion weakened Coffin's resistance. Also, he and Katie kept praying for guidance. "The free-labor stores are striking a blow against slavery, and I want to help them," said Levi.

154

FINALLY the Coffins sold their business in Newport, rented their home, and moved to Cincinnati on April 22, 1847. A large brick building that had been erected for a convent was secured for both the business and their living quarters.

As Levi showed Catherine through the substantial building, he kept pointing out the maze of secret passages and hidden rooms. "We're better equipped here for Underground Railroad work than we were in Newport," he said.

Business at the depot was brisk and it was hard to keep enough supplies to service the growing orders adequately and efficiently, for only goods manufactured by free labor qualified. Searching for a solution, Levi came in contact with a William McCray who lived near Holly Springs in northern Mississippi. From him and others, Levi learned that most of the farmers in this area employed only free labor.

Excited by this discovery, Levi arranged for a cotton gin to be shipped down to him. This thirty-saw machine was dubbed the Abolition Gin and arrangements were made to purchase all the free cotton that could be economically shipped to it.

Through this method, more and more free cotton was shipped to Levi Coffin in Cincinnati.

Because of his business Levi Coffin made many trips into the South. By this time his Underground Railroad activities were well known, and yet through the force of his Christian character, and because of the tolerance of those who opposed him, he was never insulted nor hindered. Indeed, he was often asked to give lectures on slavery and, when he could, he complied.

THE COFFINS had not lived in Cincinnati long until wagons began to pull up in the middle of the night and ask them to hide the passengers and forward them to the next station. Here Levi did not have surplus wagons and horses such as he had had in Newport, nor was he surrounded with friendly Quakers who knew when to help and when to close their eyes. And so when transportation for slaves was needed, Coffin had to hire the wagon and horses — usually for $10. Since he frequently had to hire as many as three wagons at a time, his expenses were heavy.

Partly to meet these expenses, and partly because he could not stand waste, Levi opened his house to boarders. Even so, the house was so large, and the secret rooms were so secure, the boarders were seldom aware of the hidden fugitives. Sometimes the hidden people were right under the feet of the men and women who lodged in the big house. Occasionally a boarder witnessed a scene that he was not supposed to see.

One afternoon Catherine hurried to the window. She squinted from behind a curtain and then motioned to her husband. "Levi," she said, "look! The marshall is coming down the street, and there are two men with him. I think he's coming here. Yes, he is. Hurry!"

Levi rushed out of the door and met the trio at the gate. The window was open and she could hear their conversation.

"Good afternoon, Friend Coffin," said the official. "We are seeking two runaways."

"You mean two escaped slaves you would like to recapture?" asked Levi.

"Yes, yes," replied the trio, speaking as one voice.

"Hmm," mused Coffin. his chin in hand. "Was one boy black and rather heavyset, and the other mulatto and slightly built?"

"Yes! Yes!" exclaimed the owners. "They're the ones!"

"I saw such boys not half an hour ago. They passed through this very gate. They wanted to know where the Cincinnati, Hamilton, and Dayton depot was." He glanced quickly at his watch. "If you men hurry, you can reach the depot before the train leaves."

With this information burning their ears, the men took off for the depot on the double.

Returning to the parlor with a sly grin, Levi said, "Mark my word, Katie, I only said the boys 'passed through this very gate.' But I did not mention which way they passed! Hurry up and feed them so that I can hitch up the old bay horse and get them to a station down the way."

BY THE late 1840s, so many slaves were escaping to the free states and Canada, the South was alarmed. The Fugitive Slave Act of 1793 was still in effect, but the slaveholders did not think it was strong enough to protect their "property." By 1850, the South was determined that the Thirty-first Congress would come up with a new law — one with solid, sharp fangs in it.

In an early session of Congress, Mr. Mason of Virginia declared that under the existing law, "you may as well go down to the sea and endeavor to recover from his native element a fish which has escaped from you, as to expect to recover such a fugitive. Every difficulty is thrown in your way by the population. . . . There are armed mobs [and] rescues. This is the real state of things."

The new bill, which was introduced by Mason on January 4, was hotly debated and amended again and again. Both the North and the South followed its progress with keen interest. Newspapers headlined the story day after day. When there were unexpected developments, newsboys swarmed the streets shouting, "Extra! Extra! Read all about it!"

Many abolitionists hoped that President Zachary Taylor would veto the new bill if it managed to squirm through the House and Senate. And then, unexpectedly, Taylor died of typhoid on July 9. His successor was Vice-President Millard Fillmore.

The bill came to a vote in the House on September 12 and was passed by a lopsided margin of 109 to 75. The measure breezed through the Senate without difficulty and was signed into law by President Fillmore on September 18.

Southern newspapers gloated over the law, while Northern newspapers denounced it as a "villainous act worthy of the devil."

The moment the Fugitive Slave Law of 1850, as it came to be known, was available in print, Levi Coffin secured a copy. After trimming and turning up the lamp, he seated himself by the fireplace and began to study it. As his eyes devoured the lines, he became more and more angry.

"What's the matter?" asked Catherine. "You're face is white."

"It's this wicked slave law," said Levi. "I've followed

it carefully in the papers, and I knew what it would be like. But now that I have it in my hands, I can see that it's even worse than I thought."

"How can that be?"

"The whole law, every word, comma, jot, and tittle is for the benefit of the slaveholder! The slaveholder, or his agent, can seize a black person — any black person — and take him before a judge or commissioner and claim him as his property or the property of his employer.

"If the officer doesn't think there is enough evidence to hold the person, his fee is $5. But if he turns the accused over to the accuser his fee is $10! The poor black doesn't have a chance. Let me read you the exact words from section 6." He ran his eyes down the page until he found it. "Here, it is. 'In no trial or hearing under this act shall the testimony of such alleged fugitive be admitted to evidence.'"

"In other words, the accused cannot defend himself," said Katie.

"That's right. Any white man can accuse almost any black and the poor fellow doesn't have any more chance than a lame canary at a tomcat convention!"

"What happens to those who help the fugitives?" asked Katie.

"I was afraid you'd get to that. But before I read it, you'd better sit down. Here it is in section 7. Look, I've underlined it. The one who helps a fugitive will be 'subject to a fine not exceeding one thousand dollars, and imprisonment not exceeding six months.' But that isn't all. At the bottom of the paragraph it says that the one who has helped the fugitive shall pay

159

'by way of civil damages to the party injured . . . the sum of one thousand dollars for each fugitive lost.' "

"In other words the owners of those seventeen we helped escape could demand seventeen thousand dollars from us," said Katie.

"You are absolutely right!"

"What will happen to our runaway friends who live in Cabin Creek and other such places?"

"They'll be in trouble," said Levi grimly. "And unless I'm grievously mistaken, they're heading for Canada right now! At least that's what I'd do if I were one of them. They can't defend themselves and so they don't have any protection."

"And what are we to do?" asked Katie, after she had adjusted the wick in the lamp.

"We'll do as we've always done. We'll help every fugitive who comes to our door! God will protect us. Anyway, I've already noticed a legal way to get around the law."

"And how is that?"

"It's simple. In order to condemn a person who helps a fugitive, it has to be proved that the one who helped the fugitive *knew* that the person was a fugitive. But how is he to know that if a slave's testimony cannot be accepted in court?"

"You used that argument at Centerville when they accused you of helping the seventeen runaways, didn't you?"

"That's right, and it will work again — even under the new law!"

INTRIGUE

LEVI WAS sorting the mail when he heard the crunch of steps approaching the front door. Assuming that it was the milkman, he continued with the mail which had been unusually heavy that morning.

He had just placed the current issue of the *National Era* on one side of his desk and a thick letter from Jonathan Greene on the other side, when there was a firm knock at the door.

"Mt. Hatfield wants to see you at his house immediately," said the young out-of-breath messenger.

Levi glanced at his watch. "It's only 7:29!"

"I know. But it's very important."

"I hated to bother you," said John Hatfield after he had carefully locked his door. "But we decided that you are the only one in Cincinnati who could help us."

Circling the living room some of the leading black men of the city, and sitting at the table in the kitchen was the always-intense John Fairfield. Fairfield, covered with grime, was devouring his breakfast with the zest of one on the verge of starvation.

Speaking around a mouthful of toast, Fairfield said, "I've just brought twenty-eight fugitives into the area! We crossed the Ohio at Lawrenceburg, Indiana. Now we've got to get them out of here and on their way to Canada — "

"Where are they?"

"I hid them in some ravines just outside the city."

"If there were only a dozen of them we wouldn't have much trouble," said Hatfield. "But trying to take twenty-eight slaves across this town in the middle of the day is like trying to walk through a tiger's cage and not get scratched."

A number of plans were suggested by the group, but each one was turned down. Suddenly Levi's face brightened. "I've thought of a plan that will work" he said with confidence.

"Let's hire a couple of funeral coaches and line them up on the road to Cumminsville. Then you men," he pointed to the blacks, "can go over to the place where the fugitives are hidden and drive them in buggies up to the funeral coaches. When all the coaches are lined up with the buggies, the whole procession can continue solemnly along the road. No one will be suspicious since the Methodist Church has a burial ground for blacks on the west side of Cumminsville."

"And what will we do when we get to the burial ground?" asked a thin-faced black, leaning forward.

"When you get there, just keep going. You see as you are going toward the cemetery, the slave-catchers will think that you are going *to* a funeral. As you continue, they will think you are returning *from* one."

"Very good so far," said Fairfield, frowning. "But what do we do with the buggies — and what do we do with the slaves?"

"Simple," replied Levi. He sketched a map on the back of an envelope. "The procession will continue on the Colerain pike until it reaches the road leading to College Hill. Turn there and keep going toward Farmer's College. A Presbyterian preacher by the name of Jonathan Cable lives near this place. He's an abolitionist and he'll arrange for the blacks in the area to care for the fugitives."

John Hatfield agreed to the plan at once. "I know Cable well. I'll go on ahead and tell him to be ready."

"And I'll make a lunch of coffee and sandwiches for the runaways," volunteered Mrs. Hatfield. "You can take it to them in one of the buggies."

Miraculously, the rather complicated plan worked. As the solemn procession serpentined along the road to and beyond the cemetery, some whom they passed even removed their hats in honor of the "deceased."

Yet there was tragedy. Sick from overexposure, a baby began to cry. The mother squeezed it close and wrapped a blanket around herself and the infant. Soon the baby quieted and she assumed he was asleep. But when the blanket was removed, it was discovered that the tiny fragment of humanity was dead.

The local blacks kindly arranged for the baby's funeral. The fugitives stayed hidden with their hosts for several days. When it was thought to be safe, they

163

were smuggled into an Underground Railroad station and sent on their way. Levi arranged their route by the way of Hamilton, West Elkton, and Eaton, Ohio; to Newport, Indiana. Eventually the entire group reached Canada and Levi received a letter from them expressing their thankfulness.

WHEN LEVI returned home, Katie met him at the door. "I've hidden a couple of runaways," she said excitedly. "But the police are suspicious. They're on the way right now to get a search warrant from the judge. And so when they come, be ready."

As Levi awaited the police, he opened Jonathan Greene's letter. Again it was full of clippings about the arrest and punishment of abolitionists. Levi spread the items out on his desk to read. The longest one was about a Mr. Booth who had been convicted of helping a fugitive. He was fined $1,000 and had to pay $1,451 in costs. Levi had just started to read the next one when the police arrived.

"I am Sergeant O'Keefe," said the burly one, "and here's our search warrant. We want to look for a pair of slaves."

"Go ahead, and when you get through I'll ask Katie to pour you some coffee."

The men went from room to room. Levi could hear the sound of beds being moved and of closets being searched. After about an hour, O'Keefe faced Levi. "Well, where are they?" he asked.

"What do you mean by they?"

"The slave girls."

"Didn't you find them?"

"You know we didn't."

"Did you look inside the oven? And how about the stovepipe? It's only about six inches across. But one never knows!"

As O'Keefe started to leave, Levi said, "Aren't you going to stay for coffee? We'd enjoy having a chance to visit."

A MONTH later, O'Keefe and three or four other officers began to patrol the streets around Coffin's house. Slightly annoyed, Levi went up to the sergeant. "You know there's a saying that time is money. You've been here for three days and so you've wasted a lot of money."

"It's our duty, sir," replied O'Keefe, his voice coldly correct.

"I feel sorry for a man who is willing to hunt down his fellow human beings in order to make a living. Such a person must be in dire distress."

"But, Mr. Coffin, the owners of these slaves have paid good money for them. If your horse ran off you'd want it returned, wouldn't you?"

"You're quite right. But there's a vast difference between a man and a horse. Incidentally, do you take the *National Era*?"

"I don't think so," he replied, rubbing his chin.

"You should. There's a great serial running in it right now. It's by Harriet Beecher Stowe, and it's called *Uncle Tom's Cabin*. Indeed, I'm going into the house right now so that I can read the last installment. Are you sure you don't want a cup of coffee?"

"Not today, Mr. Coffin."

CANADA

OTHER than the Bible, there was no reading material
in the Coffin home as popular as Mrs. Stowe's long
serial in the *National Era*. This eight-page newspaper,
published in Washington, D.C., proclaimed the cause of
abolitionism and was considered a must by all those
who worked against slavery.

The "Uncle Tom's Cabin" serial began appearing
on May 8, 1851. The Coffins read every word of it, as
did subscribers all over America and Canada. Fan mail
poured into the publisher's offices. Editor Bailey was
so excited by the response, he printed one of the
letters — an almost unheard of thing in that day. The
reader wrote:

> Uncle Tom's Cabin increases in interest and pathos
> with each successive number. None of thy various contribu-
> tions, rich and varied as they have been, have so deeply

interested thy female readers of this vicinity as this story of Mrs. Stowe has so far done and promises to do.

The words "this vicinity" referred to the fact that the number of readers far surpassed the circulation. Many of the issues were literally worn out as they passed from hand to hand.

From the time "Eliza" first appeared in the serial, Catherine began to wonder if this was the Eliza who had spent time with them in Newport. And the more she read, the more convinced she became. Many of the incidents in the lives of both women — including the crossing of the Ohio on the ice — were almost identical.

If she had any doubts at all, however, they vanished when she read the thirteenth installment entitled, "The Quaker Settlement." "We're in the serial!" she exclaimed an hour after the latest *National Era* had arrived. "Our new names are Rachel and Simeon Halliday." *

"I think you're right," agreed Levi after he had read the installment. "But Mrs. Stowe thinks you are older than you really are. She says you are fifty-five or sixty!"

"That's all right," laughed Katie. "I'm mighty proud to have been the model for such a fine woman as Rachel Halliday."

IN THE SUMMER of 1854, the Coffins had the opportunity to visit Canada along with Laura S. Haviland

---

*Scholars are almost universally agreed that the Eliza who hid with the Coffins in Newport is the Eliza of *Uncle Tom's Cabin* and that the Coffins were the models for Simeon and Rachel Halliday. Harriet Beecher Stowe had lived in Cincinnati for years and probably knew the Coffins.

— a Michigan lady who had established a school for fugitives about eight miles south of Windsor, Ontario. While attending a black congregation, a slendor quadroon almost ran up to the Coffins.

"How are you, Aunt Katie?" she exclaimed, taking both of Catherine's hands in both of hers.

Catherine looked at her doubtfully. "I'm sorry, but I don't think I know you."

"Oh sure you do, Aunt Katie. I'm Eliza!"

"And so you are," Katie almost shouted. "But you've changed. You look better and — and — and you've gained a little weight."

"A tiny, tiny favor, Aunt Katie?"

"If I can."

"Could you come down and visit us at Chatham? We've built a little cabin and Lewis would love to see you."

"We'll be there. Just name the time," promised Levi with enthusiasm.

THE SMALL frame house was tastefully furnished. Vines shaded the window and a miniature garden by the side was aflame with brilliant red roses, marigolds, and bachelor's buttons. Two little boys were wrestling on the floor when the Coffins entered.

"And where is Harry?" asked Katie.

"Oh, he's a big boy now. He's in school. He and my husband will be home at noon."

After several minutes of excited small talk, Levi Coffin said, "Eliza, I've always wondered how you made it to Canada."

"My escape was a miracle. We had no trouble at all.

But when we got to Sandusky, I had a strong feeling that I'd better put on a disguise: and so I dressed as a man. It's good that I did, for as I was mounting the steps to the boat, I saw my owner. He was searching all over the dock and watching those who entered the ship. He looked in my direction several times, but he didn't recognize me."

"And how did you find your husband?" asked Catherine.

"That wasn't as hard as it might seem. The former slaves up here have a way of passing on information about one another and newly arrived slaves."

Suddenly the door opened, and there stood Lewis and Harry. "And so you're Aunt Katie and Uncle Levi," Lewis said. "Eliza has been telling me about you ever since she escaped."

After an excellent dinner of roast beef, the Coffins were ready to leave when Eliza came up with a box of cookies. "Remember that recipe I gave you at Newport? Well here are some cookies made by that recipe. And please, whenever you come to Canada, drop in and see us."

AT ANOTHER meeting, a white-headed old man went up to Katie. " 'Member me?" he asked.

After careful study of his bent form, she shook her head. "I'm sorry. I'm afraid I don't."

"La me!" he exclaimed, "Misses, don't you 'member when dey was close after to take me and you hid me in de feather bed and saved me? Why, bress your heart! If it hadn't been for you I should nebber been here. It's more den twenty years ago, and my head is

169

white and my back is bent, but I hasn't forgòt dat time."

With these reminders, the Coffins remembered him. The old man's eyes glowed when they shared the happenings of that crisis day in his life. Others also came and reminded the Coffins of their help.

On First Day of the eighth month, the Coffins attended a special meeting which was called to celebrate emancipation in the West Indies. After the meeting, a slender young black came up to them.

"Sam!" said Levi, shaking his hand vigorously.

"So you remember me," cried Sam, almost beside himself.

"Of course. You were engaged to Uncle Frank's daughter, and when Catherine and I were leaving North Carolina you came out with the preacher and sang for us. Also, it was your master who sliced off the top of your ear. Right?"

"Yes, that's right."

"Tell me, did you marry Uncle Frank's daughter?"

"Yes, we were married — but not legally, you know, the way free people do. But as soon as Suzi escapes and gets up here we're gonna have a regular church weddin'."

"And how is Uncle Frank?"

"Didn't you hear? Well, you know Dr. Caldwell died the year you moved to Indiana. Uncle Frank was then inherited by one of the sons. And that son was good to him. He even allowed him to keep preachin'. And when his rheumatism got so bad he couldn't walk, his massa kept sendin' people to take care of him.

"Uncle Frank sure loved you and Missi Catherine. He

prayed for you every day. When he heard dat you were helpin' the slaves get to Canada, he was shore happy. I was with him when he died. He'd always wanted to send you somethin', but bein' a slave he didn't have no money. And so do you know what he did?"

"No, do tell me."

"When he knowed he was gonna die, he said to me. 'Sam, turn my head to de norf so dat when I'se dead I'll be facin' Levi Coffin!'

"And so when de end was near, I arranged his bed so that he was a-lookin' to de norf. And I guess I did it just in time, for he took a deep breath or two and den he was gone. But, Mistah Coffin, you should have seen de look of joy that was on his face! Yes, he was a good man; and he loved you. He said dat you was the nearest to being just like Jesus of any man he'd ever seen."

THE
SUMMING UP

AS "Uncle Tom's Cabin" neared completion in the *National Era,* Mrs. Stowe's sister, Catherine Beecher, secured permission to offer the book rights to her own publisher — Phillips, Sampson & Co. This Boston firm had done well with Catherine's book, *True Remedy,* and Catherine felt certain they would take "Uncle Tom."

Catherine was mistaken.

The book was promptly refused. "It will not sell a thousand copies," predicted one of the partners.

Mrs. John P. Jewett of Boston, however, had enjoyed the serial and insisted that her husband publish it. Jewett frowned at this suggestion. His specialty was "practical" books, not fiction. Nevertheless, he decided to take a chance. Before the contract was signed, he approached the Stowes with the suggestion that they pay half the printing costs and then share in half the profits.

172

But, since the Stowes were nearly penniless, they decided to take a 10 percent royalty. This seemed the sensible thing to do, for Mrs. Stowe's wildest hope was that the book would earn her enough to buy a new silk dress.

The two-volume book make its appearance in March 1852. It was published in both cloth and paper. It sold for $1.00 in paper, $1.50 in cloth, and in "full-gilt" was available at $2.00 "with discount to the trade." A mere 5,000 copies were printed in the first edition and not a single prepublication review copy was mailed out.

Few knowledgeable people thought the book would sell. A first novel by a poor professor's wife — and on slavery? Impossible!

But the public was ready for a book about Eliza, Uncle Tom, Little Eva, and Rachel and Simeon Halliday. Twenty thousand copies were gobbled up in the first three weeks! And from this point, sales and translations zoomed. Soon *Uncle Tom's Cabin* was being read around the world in nearly forty languages.

The success of this book had a remarkable effect on Levi Coffin — and all abolitionists. No longer were they scorned with the intensity that they had been scorned. Moreover citizens — even influential citizens — everywhere, in both the North and the South, began to speak out against slavery and the Fugitive Slave Law of 1850.

More "Liberty Laws" were hurried through legislatures in most of the Northern states. These laws were in direct contradiction to the new Federal law. They forbade the placing of Negro fugitives in state jails and they prohibited state judges and officers from issuing writs or giving help to claimants who sought to recover their slaves.

The states expected these laws to be obeyed, and they listed penalties for those who did not obey them. In most of the states, the penalty varied from a $500 fine to six months in jail. Vermont, however, was more severe. There the maximum punishment was a $2,000 fine and ten years in prison!

Levi and Catherine continued their Underground Railroad work — and watched the papers, for a coming conflict seemed inevitable. They were horrified when John Brown, on the night of October 16, 1859, seized the Federal arsenal at Harper's Ferry. Levi appreciated Brown's zeal to free the slaves, but he did not approve of violence. "The Lord has other ways of getting His work done," he said sorrowfully.

Three years before this, the division among the Society of Friends in Indiana had ended. They united their meetings, and the old quarrel over the right way to end slavery was over. This healing had been achieved through love and understanding, and Levi felt the same methods would work with slavery.

Everyone, however, seemed to know that a showdown on slavery was coming. John Brown's raid failed and he was subsequently hanged. Nevertheless, it has been estimated that the raid devalued the slaves in Virginia by $10,000,000. The pillars that supported the institution of slavery were rotting — and the slaveholders knew it!

When, on the election of Abraham Lincoln as President in 1860 South Carolina seceded from the Union,

Levi Coffin was deeply grieved. "This isn't the solution," he said to Katie again and again. But the prayers and hopes of those who were against war seemed in vain. Fort Sumter was attacked on April 12, 1861, and the War Between the States which was to snuff out the lives of more than half a million men became a grim reality.

In spite of the war, fugitives — many from Kentucky — continued to knock on Levi's door. All of them were welcome, and their needs were met. The sewing circle which had been organized for this purpose kept busy. Frequently runaways, and occasionally free blacks, needed legal help. To meet this need, Levi Coffin engaged the services of Rutherford B. Hayes — an attorney who had opened a law office in Cincinnati in 1850. A friend of the oppressed, Hayes was always ready to help. In addition, he served without charge.

AS THE WAR which many had believed would end within a few weeks spread and deepened, concerned churches in Cincinnati announced special union prayer meetings to pray for peace.

In this period, John G. Fee, one of Coffin's business friends from Berea, Kentucky, spent the night with him in Cincinnati. The next day, Fee suggested that they go to one of these prayer meetings. Coffin had already been to one, and was disappointed; but he was quite willing to go to another with his friend.

The modest hall was crowded with businessmen. A chairman, armed with a mallet, presided. One after another rose to his feet and spoke. There were prayers, confessions, and words of encouragement. But no one mentioned the sin of slavery, and Levi Coffin was deeply disturbed.

Then impulsive John G. Fee got to his feet and proceeded to denounce slavery. As he spoke, there was a great uneasiness throughout the hall. The chairman gently tapped his mallet. Fee, however, ignored the chairman as he outlined the sin of buying and selling another human being.

Desperate by now, the chairman began to thump his mallet louder. Finally Fee stopped, but on his return to his seat, he sank to his knees and in a loud voice implored the Lord to forgive the nation for tolerating slavery. He also begged the Lord to withhold His judgment on the nation's sins.

As Levi and Fee were leaving the hall, they were met with a lot of sullen faces and staring eyes. And then Horace Bushnell, one of America's great theologians, stepped up. Grasping Fee by the hand, he said, "Brother Fee, you drove in the nail and then you clinched it, and they can't get it out."

"It is strange," said Levi Coffin on the way home, "how people will confess every sin except the sin that is causing the trouble. Friend Fee, I was mighty proud of you!"

NEWS THAT Confederate General Kirby Smith was going to attack Cincinnati spread through the county with lightning speed. The mayor issued a proclamation that every man in the city was to register and help defend it.

Levi Coffin refused to comply. When he was faced by an officer who threatened to arrest him, he said, "I am

176

nonresistant. I could not take a gun and go out and shoot anybody. That is contrary to the spirit and doctrines of the gospel."

The law threatened force, but Coffin refused to budge. He did, however, allow wounded soldiers to be treated in his house. And finally, because of his reputation and the force of his character, he was allowed to remain in his home without registering for military service.

Thousands of slaves fled to the Union lines. Many of them were placed on boats and sent to several points along the river. Quite often the wharves at Cincinnati were packed with these helpless people who were provided with neither food nor shelter. Many were old and in rags. Levi worked with others to secure shelter and food for them. The city and the Union commanders were most cooperative. Levi even managed to help provide a school and religious services for the slaves. Attending one of these services, Levi was impressed by the enthusiastic singing of the recently freed blacks. He declared it was the greatest singing that he had ever heard.

All along, Levi had insisted that the only way to settle the war was to free the slaves. "We cannot have God's blessings when there is sin in the camp," he said. When the slaves were freed through the Emancipation Proclamation which was signed on September 22, 1863, he predicted that the conflict would soon be over. In this, he was mistaken, for the war dragged on until Lee's surrender on April 9, 1865.

The freeing of the slaves, however, brought new responsibilities to Levi Coffin. As the slaves were freed, escaped, or were abandoned, they found themselves destitute. Many starved. Along with others, Coffin helped found the Western Freedmen's Aid Commission. This organization gathered food and supplies for the freed slaves. Coffin became their general agent, and as a result often had to go through the Federal lines into the South to help the former slaves. General Grant gave him free rail transportation, and the Society of Friends along with many other denominations raised money and brought in supplies.

In 1864, Coffin went to England in behalf of the Commission. He was received with enthusiasm everywhere, and especially among the Friends. Many of England's great, including John Bright, the eloquent Friend who was later to serve in Gladstone's cabinet, went to hear him and support his cause. He was featured at the famed Exeter Hall in London and 5,000 gathered to hear him. Although he was hoarse from a bad cold at the time, he did his best to represent the cause of the freed slave and to relate what the Western Freedman's Aid Commission was doing for them.

The *Evening Star* carried long quotes from his address and England responded with generous financial support.

Back in America, Coffin continued his work. He went on speaking tours, raised money, and made trips into the South. In most places where it was announced that he would speak, crowds filled the auditoriums. The story of his Underground Railroad work had spread and some of the very people who had condemned him, now came to praise him.

In 1870, when the Negroes of Cincinnati gathered to celebrate the passage of the Fifteenth Amendment to the Constitution — the one which guaranteed their right to vote — Levi decided that this was the proper time to resign from the presidency of the Underground Railroad. Accordingly, he arranged to be on the platform during the celebrations.

After the last speech had been made, Levi stepped up to the podium. He explained how he had been named president by the slavehunters, and reported that approximately three thousand slaves had passed through his station. Then he said, "The stock of the Underground Railroad has gone down on the market. The business is spoiled. The road is of no further use. And because of this, I hereby resign my position."

This statement brought many smiles and a thundering applause.

THE COFFINS moved to Avondale — a suburb of Cincinnati. Here Levi retired and began to work on his famous biography — *The Reminiscences of Levi Coffin.* °

Composing the book was a source of great pleasure. Day after day the past kept coming before him. Sometimes the dates were hazy, but the main story of the Underground Railroad had been etched firmly in his mind. The words leaped from his pen in a torrent.

The Coffins had suffered some persecution, and they had had their sorrows. Four of their children — Addison, Thomas, Anna, and Sarah — had passed away. But there had also been many joys. And in these de-

---

°Many books were published by participants of the Underground Railroad, but Levi Coffin's is considered to be among the most trustworthy. It was reprinted by Arno Press and the *New York Times* in 1968.

clining years many a black whom Levi and Catherine had helped came to express his thanks. The book was finished in Levi's seventy-eighth year at a time when his health was severely declining.

Uncle Levi and Aunt Katie had great pleasure in following the career of Rutherford B. Hayes — the attorney who had been such a help to them when they were engaged in Underground Railroad work in Cincinnati. They rejoiced when he was elected to Congress, cheered when he became the governor of Ohio, and held their breath when he was nominated President of the United States.

The results of the election were so close they were severely contested. But eventually, through a bargain with the South, Hayes was proclaimed President of the United States. The Coffins considered this a personal victory. President Hayes was a man after their own heart. Smoking, drinking, dancing, lawn parties, and card-playing were all forbidden in the White House. The one quarrel they had with him was that he was a military man!

After the election, Levi's health continued to deteriorate. He passed away on September 16, 1877. He was seventy-nine.

The funeral was conducted at the Friends Meetinghouse at the corner of Eighth and Mound Street in Avondale. Many of his co-workers were on the platform. Mr. Murray Shipley read the lesson and commented on the passage, "He went about doing good, for God was with him."

Burial was at the Quaker cemetery on West Fork near Cumminsville. Many appreciative articles were published about Levi Coffin all over America.

One of the world's truly great men had passed on. Fortunately, however, those things he had set out to do had been accomplished.

THE AUTHOR

Charles Ludwig was born on January 8, 1918, in McComb, Illinois. He went with his missionary parents to Kenya in 1927 and remained with them on the field until 1937.

Upon returning to the United States, he enrolled at Anderson College where he was graduated with a bachelor's degree. While still in college, he married Mary Puchek.

Shortly after his return to America, Charles Ludwig

entered a writing contest sponsored by Warner Press. He won first prize — ten dollars' worth of books! Since then, he has published over a thousand articles, short stories, serials, and nearly three dozen books. His writings have appeared in ten languages.

In addition to writing, Charles Ludwig has pastored five congregations and has conducted over three hundred evangelistic campaigns. He has preached in many countries around the world. In recognition of his preaching and writing, Gulf Coast Bible College awarded him a Doctor of Divinity degree in 1973.

The Ludwigs have two children — both of them high school teachers.